CO   11-06-97

TELL ME

A Book about Storytelling

Joseph Bruchac

HARCOURT BRACE & COMPANY

SAN DIEGO • NEW YORK • LONDON

Library of Congress Cataloging-in-Publication Data
Bruchac, Joseph, 1942–
Tell me a tale: a book about storytelling/Joseph Bruchac.
p.   cm.
Includes bibliographical references.
Summary: Storyteller Joseph Bruchac incorporates many of his favorite
tales in this discussion of the four basic components of storytelling:
listening, observing, remembering, and sharing.
ISBN 0-15-201221-4
1. Tales.   2. Storytelling—Juvenile literature.
[1. Storytelling.   2. Folklore.]
I.Title.
GR74.B78   1997
808.5'43—dc20   96-21697

Text set in Adobe Caslon Regular
Designed by Ivan Holmes
First edition
A C E F D B
Printed in the United States of America

For my grandparents,
whose stories started me down this road

CONTENTS

STORIES USED IN THE BOOK

INTRODUCTION

Few things have helped me understand the world better than a good story. People have always listened to stories, and it seems we were born to be listeners. Little Loon, one of my Abenaki elders, told me that is why our Creator made us with two ears and only one mouth. We're supposed to listen twice as much as we talk. And with two ears, we can hear things from more than one side—especially when those things are stories. You've probably noticed how almost everyone starts to listen as soon as someone says, "Do you want to hear a story?" The best storytellers will tell you that they have listened to far more stories than they have told.

I'm now a professional storyteller and writer, but long before that I was a young person listening to stories. Stories helped me to grow, and stories helped me gain insight. (Stories are still helping me to grow and gain insight!) Stories have been a part of my life since my childhood, and they have been an important part of the lives of my own children. Stories helped me overcome my problems and stories taught me many things: that I didn't have to be ashamed when I was afraid, that I could learn to be brave, that there were times for sorrow and times for joy, that things were always going to change, and that some things—like love and courage, hope and faith—were unchanging. I learned through hearing stories that I had my own stories to tell, and that if I told them well, people would want to hear them.

Stories also taught me that things don't always happen as quickly as you want them to happen. By sharing some of my stories of growing up and some of the stories that have continued to teach me, by telling you about the kinds of storytelling, I hope to help you see the many ways stories can be a part of your life. Stories can connect you to a circle that never ends.

Many years ago one of my teachers was a Mohegan Indian elder named Harold Tantaquidgeon. I do not mean that he taught a class I took in school. He was a person who tried to teach the many people he met, to share his knowledge with them, to show them things they needed to know. If you are lucky, you will meet such teachers in your life, too.

One of the things Harold Tantaquidgeon showed me helped me to understand that circle which never ends. He and his sister Gladys ran a small American Indian museum in the town of Uncasville, Connecticut. On the wall of their museum Harold had drawn a cross with four dots placed on it like this:

Harold explained to me that this was his personal sign. That personal sign stands for many things. One of the most important ones is that we all have four grandparents. We need to look back to those two older men and those two older women because their stories have much to teach us.

I believe this to be very true for everyone. It's been said that history repeats itself, and the lessons our grandparents learned, even though the world seems to be constantly changing, are often lessons that can be useful for us today. Learning the stories of our grandparents is especially important for those of us who are interested in telling stories.

The four dots also stand for the never-ending circle of life. As we move around that circle, there are certain things we must do if we are to learn and grow and live a good life. The first step is to listen. If we do not listen, then we will hear nothing. The second step is to observe. If we do not look carefully at things, then we will not really see them. The third step is to remember. If we do not remember those things we have learned, then we have learned nothing. The fourth step is to share. If we do not share, then the circle does not continue. If we place the circle around those four points, it looks like this:

The teaching about the circle of learning is so important to me that I have used it as the structure for this book. Together we can listen, observe, and remember. And from those things we hear and see and keep in our memory, we can begin to share. Sharing is what stories are all about. And stories can be used in many different ways. Sometimes you might want to just hear a story. Sometimes telling a story is what you need to do. It might be a story you remember, or it might even be a new story that has never been told before, one that you invent yourself. You can write your stories down, or you can tell them orally. Whichever way you choose to use a story, that story can be like a good friend, right there with you when it is needed.

Stories can help us find our way home. When I was in grade school I first heard an ancient Greek story about a hero named Theseus. He found his way out of a dangerous maze by following a thread. That thread was very small, but it showed him the way to go.

Stories can bring enjoyment into our lives. They can even get us to laugh at ourselves. One of my favorite Abenaki stories tells how the mighty hero Gluskabe was defeated by a tiny baby when he could not make the infant stop crying.

We each need to find and follow our own thread of stories. We need to travel that road of danger and laughter, of mystery and understanding, which has always been the road of stories. Perhaps *Tell Me a Tale* will help you take one small step on that journey into stories, stories that will enrich your journey and last your entire life.

I hope that will be so.

A Note to Parents

As a parent of two sons, I found stories extremely useful during the years they were growing up. When I wanted to share my experiences with them, I did it through stories. When I wanted to help them understand that some of the things they wanted to do were dangerous, I used stories. I found that a cautionary story has more long-term effect than simply saying, "Don't do that!" and then when your child asks "Why?" answering, "Because I said so!" There is always the possibility that even if you tell your child not to do something, there very well may come a time when you are not around to oversee him or her and that child will do exactly what he or she was told not to do! But a well-told, memorable story will remain with a child, and it may be the one thing that will remind that child of the consequences he or she might face when doing something dangerous. My two sons, Jim and Jesse, are grown men now. Both of them are storytellers who work with young children. When they talk about their own childhoods, they remember the stories they were told, and they remember times when those stories helped them make the right decision when their parents were not around. They believe in the truth of stories.

There has never been a time when we have been more in need of the truth to be found in stories. The stories most young people hear every day are those told on television, in the movies, and in video games. In those stories success and justice are often based on power and revenge. If someone does something bad to the hero, he just goes out and seeks revenge on others in his way. I believe that there's an atmosphere of violence around us that makes people afraid. And when people are afraid, they sometimes do violent things themselves. I've talked to a lot of young people who've told me that they belong to gangs because as members of a gang, which is like a family that will protect them, they feel safer.

Stories can teach us ways to solve problems by means other than violence. Sometimes the person who seems like an enemy can even be turned into a friend. Many of the stories in the New Testament tell about people considered bad who became followers and friends of Jesus Christ. When I was young, I was smaller than the other boys and I was often bullied. My grandmother told me those Bible stories many times. They helped me see that it was possible for love to cast out fear.

I learned a similar lesson from American Indian traditions. The Iroquois are a league of five Native American nations of the Northeast. One of their most powerful stories tells of a time when five nations were killing one another in blood feuds. It was like gang warfare. If they harmed one of us, then we had to harm one of them. Then a messenger was sent by the Creator. That messenger was a man who was a storyteller. He was called the Peacemaker, and his stories showed the Iroquois nations how to end their fighting and form a League of Peace.

One of the best things about telling stories to your children is that you may also find those stories useful to you in your own lives as adults. Stories help us form identity. In the world of oneness that we find ourselves moving toward, things may sometimes become too homogenized—just as every town and city in America seems to have the same restaurants and the same movies playing in its theaters. There is nothing wrong with shared experience, but we need personal identities to succeed and to fully enjoy our world. We need the richness of family and village stories, of alternative styles of dress and music and dance, different spiritual and cultural traditions. We want to know how things might be done differently in the world. Hearing and knowing our stories will help us keep those worlds of diversity and strong identity alive for us and for our children.

Stories are wonderful teachers. Storytellers will tell you that they are always learning from their stories. Stories have been friends and guides to me throughout my life. I hope that my life experience in telling stories will be useful to you.

TELL ME A TALE

1

It all begins with listening. There are stories everywhere around us, but many people don't notice those stories because they don't take the time to listen. Or if they hear a story being told that is one they've heard, they stop listening. "I've heard that before," they say. Yet if we listen closely to any story, we may hear new things almost every time it is told.

A friend of mine named Simon Ortiz is an Acoma Pueblo writer and storyteller. His father was a famous story-teller before him. One of Simon's favorite words is *listen*. I have heard him say it again and again. There are always things we can listen to, and in all of those things we can find stories. We must listen and keep listening.

Many years ago I was taught an exercise in listening by a man named Norman Russell. He called the exercise "opening the wind." Norman is a Cherokee poet, a storyteller, and a teacher of plant science. Norman explained to me that in this modern world, most people have forgotten how to listen. They only hear what they choose to hear, and what they choose to hear is a very small part of everything around them. They only hear the loudest sounds, and they miss the small ones. They hear the shouting, but they miss the whispers. And some of the best stories are whispered to us on the wind.

This is how to open the wind. First, you must find a quiet place. That isn't always easy to do, especially if you live in a big city. But find a place that is relatively quiet, a place where you are not listening to anything else, like a television. It doesn't have to be completely quiet, but it should not be in the midst of loud noises. Norman suggested sitting out on a back porch, yard, stoop, or fire escape on a summer evening, just before it gets dark. In the evening, those moments right between day and night, many things happen. The most important thing is to find a familiar place close to home where you can sit undisturbed outdoors and listen.

Imagine that there is a large circle drawn around you. Close your eyes and listen to everything within that circle. You may hear the creaking of floorboards or the chair you are sitting on. You may hear the sounds of your own breath or the rustling of your clothes. You may even hear the sound of your own heart beating.

Open your eyes and look around you. Some of the things you were hearing can be seen. Some may be hidden from your eyes, but because you have listened, you know they are there. You've just listened to the first circle of the wind. Now imagine a circle that is bigger than the first one, one that takes in things that are farther away. In a yard this may include bushes and trees. In the city this may include part of the street or even the front of another building. There may be people in this larger circle. Do not forget the things you heard in the first circle; include them in your listening and add in the new sounds. Now close your eyes and listen again. This time you may hear the wind in the tree branches or the singing of a bird. You may hear people talking, and you may be surprised at how clearly you can hear what they are saying. You may hear sounds that are always there around you but that you have never really noticed before.

You can go on making larger circles in this exercise. It takes time, but I found that after doing this exercise for a few weeks, I could hear things that were far away, from the gentle voice of the katydid in a maple tree across the street to the howl of a coyote on a distant hill. Our human ears are much better than we think they are; it is just that we spend a lot of time filling our ears with loud sounds that prevent us from hearing anything else.

Why listen to a story? A story tells us about something that happened in a way that helps us experience the event. When we hear a story, a story that is well told, we can see the story happening. Through stories we can visit places we've never been before and see things that are familiar as if they were brand-new. Stories can remind us of things we thought we had forgotten and help us relive our own past and the pasts of others.

Movies and television use lots of stories, although they use images on the screen to help tell the story. Books, comics, even music also tell us stories. In spoken or written stories, your imagination must create the pictures in your mind. In some ways, the image on a screen limits imagination. A second grader once told me he enjoyed hearing a story told more than watching television because, as he said, "The pictures are better in my mind." It may cost a million dollars to create one scene in a movie, but with imagination we can create a scene ourselves even more vividly inspired by a few well-chosen words in a story. All that is needed for story-telling is a storyteller, a listener, a shared language, and the memory of a story.

I'll talk more about the *how* of storytelling later in the book, but for now here are a few basic things to remember about stories.

○ It takes at least two people to share a story—one to tell and one to listen. The listener is a big part of the story. It is not like a television program or a movie that goes on even if the room is empty. Stories are meant to be shared between the teller and the listener. Stories are alive. Telling a story to someone else is a very special, personal experience. Having that story told to you is just as special and personal.

○ Hearing a story is like going on a journey guided by the storyteller's voice. Though there may be excitement and danger along the way, the story always brings you back home safely.

○ Stories have a beginning, a middle, and an end. You can tell when a story begins, and it is made very clear to you when a story ends. Use special words to begin and end a story. These words vary, but we all know some of them. "Once upon a time..." is a well-known beginning. "They all lived happily ever after" may be the most familiar ending.

◗ Stories are like growing, living things. You might even say that stories are like trees, with many branches.

Each story carries so many branches and leaves, so much experience and knowledge within it, that you may hear something new each time that story is told. Stories can grow with us. The stories I tell know more than I know. But the more I know, the more I am able to hear. The more I listen, really listen, the bigger that forest of stories around me becomes. And just like trees in the forest, there are many different kinds of stories.

There are funny stories, tales about tricksters such as Anansi the Spider or Coyote, who is always hungry. There are frightening stories about giants and cannibal monsters, about ghosts and buried treasures. There are stories of the sea and stories of the stars. There are stories that tell how the weak can overcome bullies, how honesty is rewarded. There are tales of elves and fairies, of flying horses and magical swords, of kings and wise women, brave girls and boys, magic lanterns and enchanted castles.

Some stories tell us how things came to be—why Bear has a short tail, how the earth was created on the back of Great Turtle. There are stories about people and stories about places, stories about things that happened not long ago, and stories about things that may never have happened—though the story makes those imagined events seem real. There are stories in songs and songs in stories. Some stories are poems, and some are like plays. And stories, like trees, have roots. They are rooted in our words and in our world.

Finding those roots can help you discover where stories live.

Where Stories Live: Where to Find Stories

Where can we find stories? First of all, each of us can listen to our own storytelling roots. Inside us we all have lots of stories about who we are, where we came from, and how our lives became what they are. It can be said that each of us has four sources for these stories, four special places to start listening. By identifying and nurturing those roots, your storytelling tree grows stronger.

YOUR STORYTELLING ROOTS

Your Ancestry: All of us have ancestors. They might be English or German, Italian or Japanese, African American or Irish, Indian or Samoan, Mexican or Vietnamese, Native American or Chinese. And there are hundreds of other ancestries here in North America. Each ancestry we have (and many of us have more than one—my own ancestry is English, Slovak, and Native American) is a source of stories and cultural traditions. There are folktales, histories, songs, and proverbs—all sorts of cultural traditions we carry with us that are part of storytelling.

Where can you find those stories? You may know some of them already. Sometimes we think that everyone knows the things that we know. I remember a little girl in Denver, Colorado, whose family came from Cambodia. She told her class the Hmong story of how Tiger disguised himself as a human to trick people so he could eat them. But a wise woman saw who Tiger was and tricked him instead. That little girl from Cambodia was surprised to find that none of the other children, who were not Hmong people like herself, knew the story. "Doesn't everyone know that story?" she asked. Remember, some of the stories you know may be old to you, but they are new to someone who has never heard them before.

Often, however, it seems that young people may not know many of the stories of their ancestors. But you are never too old to learn those stories. There are two ways to start doing this. One is to seek out written stories. Through books and computers, your librarian can help you find stories from your culture. The other thing to do is to ask your elders. Your parents or grandparents or older people who share your ancestry may know such stories and share them with you.

Your Family: We all have families, whether they are biological families, step-families, or adopted families. Every family has its own store of legends and tales. Some of us are lucky enough to have grandparents who are still living. Usually grandparents have many family stories. One kind of family story that is very common in America is the story of how your family came to where you now live. Then there are stories about what it was like when one of your older relatives was a child, stories about how people met each other and got married, stories about things that have happened in your family. Ask older relatives what stories they can tell you about your family.

You might want to make up a list of questions before you do this. Those questions might include: What was it like when you were my age? or Where did you live when you were a child? You can ask them questions about what kinds of games they played or where they went to school. Where did our family come from originally? How did people earn their living back then? You can ask them if there are stories that their own parents or grandparents told them. After you have written your list of questions, find a time when you can sit down with your grandparents or parents and ask those questions. When you do this, be patient. Sometimes you may have to ask the same question more than once. Sometimes you may get ideas for new questions because of the answers you are given. Most important of all, be a good listener.

Your Home: The place where you live has many stories connected to it. The very name of your city or town has a story, and there are many things that happened in the place where you live to know, ask, and wonder about. Your parents or grandparents may be able to tell you about some of those past happenings. Most towns or cities have had histories written about them. You can look up books of local history in your school library or your public library. My own public library, in Saratoga Springs, New York, has a special room devoted to local history called the Saratoga Room. There are also local historical societies and town historians in many communities. Such organizations and people are always willing to help young people who want to learn about local history.

Your Own Life: Things happen to us. And every life, or person, is different and has its own stories. Not all parts of life are easy. But something bad or unhappy can be less painful and easier to understand when it is made into a story. Young or old, we each have lots of stories about journeys we have taken, friends we have met, and things we have discovered. Think about it; you'll see.

Since some of the work you will be doing in tracing your storytelling roots may involve going to a library, you need to remember that what we call storytelling has been divided by scholars into different areas. Those areas include folklore, myths, legends, and literature.

Folklore is traditional knowledge passed along by word of mouth within a small isolated community of people. It may include songs, games, ways of speaking, and lore about such things as the weather or medicine, as well as myths and legends. Folklore is so old that no one knows the original author or source.

Myths are a special part of folklore. A myth is usually an ancient story that explains how things came to be long ago. It may tell of the things done by ancient gods and goddesses, such as those of Greece and Rome. Myths include the many stories of creation told around the world. One such example is the Iroquois story of how the earth was created on the back of Great Turtle. Myths are often associated with religious rites and beliefs.

Legends are also part of folklore. These are stories that are usually based on history and are said to have happened in a particular place. The English stories of King Arthur and the Knights of the Round Table or Robin Hood and his band of outlaws are examples of legends. Legends also often express the hopes and desires of a people. In the story of King Arthur, the ideas of chivalry and English standards of honor are expressed, while Robin Hood tells of the hopes of people to overcome oppression and misrule.

Literature is not part of folklore, but it is often based on folklore, myths, and legends. Literature is the writing of one particular person and—unlike with folklore—we usually know that person's name. Many literary stories, such as Washington Irving's "The Legend of Sleepy Hollow," which tells of Ichabod Crane and the headless horseman, have become so familiar that people may know the story and even tell their own versions of it without knowing the story's origin.

Generations

FAMILY STORIES

It has been said that history repeats itself. The lessons our grandparents learned, even though our world is very changed from theirs, are often lessons that can be useful to us. Learning the stories of our grandparents is especially important. Those shared memories bring together all times and all ages. Family stories hold the truths of who we are. They help us understand why certain things are important for our families. They show us how our parents and grandparents dealt with good times and bad times. Often we will find that the characteristics and personalities of our grandparents are very much like our own.

Do you have some older relative who always tells a story when he or she comes to your house? Maybe you've heard that story again and again, so often that you no longer listen to it. The story that you've heard so often might actually be a story you will want to remember years from now. There are many kinds of family stories. Here are a few examples.

Name Stories: Your family name means something. If your name is Smith, one of the most common names, it may mean one of your ancestors long ago was a blacksmith. It may also mean that your family name was changed to Smith from something else.

I have an Adirondack storyteller friend named Bill Smith, whose ancestors came from Scotland. Generations ago his family's name was MacGregor, but because the MacGregors were outlawed by the king, they changed their family name. A Jewish American friend of mine named Greg told me about a relative of his whose family name is Ding. This is an unusual last name, but that name was created by accident when one of his ancestors arrived in the United States at Ellis Island, where the immigration officials were asking names. The man ahead of Greg's relative had the same name that he did. Greg's relative spoke a little English and he was proud of that. So, when it was his turn, he thought he was ready.

"What is your name?" asked the official.

"Same ding as him," said the man, pointing at the person in front of him. He was trying to say "same *thing*," but the immigration officer heard it differently.

"Sam Ding," said the immigration official, writing it into his book.

The man tried to protest, but once it was written down,

that was that. And Ding is still the family name to this day.

Sometimes we know the meaning of our family name but may not know the exact origin of that name. My last name comes from Slovakia in Eastern Europe. Both of my father's grandparents were Slovak immigrants early in the 1900s. *Bruchac,* in Slovak, means "big belly," some say. I always laugh when I think that I am Joseph Bigbelly. In a way, that name fits me. I'm not fat, but I have a very big appetite. I have also been told that our name was originally *Bruchacek* and that its translation is not "big belly" but "little bear." Perhaps that name came to be attached to my family long ago because one of my ancestors ate like a bear.

Names have special meanings in every culture. When I lived in West Africa, I was always asking my Ghanaian friends (who belonged to the Ewe tribe) what their names meant in English. I learned that Kofi Ladzekpo was Kofi "Leopard" and that Ami Logah was Ami "Big Crocodile." I also learned that their first names had special meanings, too. In many parts of Africa, a child's first name is given according to the day of the week on which he or she was born. *Kofi* means "boy born on Friday." *Ami* means "girl born on Saturday."

Among the many different American Indian nations, in the old days, children were not given the same last name as their parents. Children might be given a nickname when they were little, but their true name would be different when they grew up. They would earn new names through the things that they did. Thus, a little Lakota boy who was called Slow when he was a child earned the name Sitting Bull as a young man after he did a deed that showed he was as brave and determined as a bull buffalo.

Here is a Native American story about names that comes from the Yakama people of the Pacific Northwest. I learned the story back in 1973 when I was visiting there with my friend Ted Palmanteer, a Yakama artist and writer. As we drove along he pointed to a hill and began to laugh. "That is Coyote's Hill," he said. "That's where he slept late."

COYOTE'S NAME

North America/Pacific Northwest/Yakama

Long ago, none of the birds or animals had names. The Creator decided to change that.

"All you animals will be given names," the Creator said. "Tomorrow, at sunrise, I will start giving you all names. The ones who get up the earliest will have the first choices."

Coyote was very excited. He began bragging to all the other birds and animals about the name he would be given. "I will get up earlier than anyone else," he said. "I will get the best name of all. Tomorrow you will know me as Eagle or Grizzly Bear. I will have a powerful name."

Coyote bragged and bragged. He talked all through the day and all through the night. The other animals and the birds went to bed, but Coyote stayed up, bragging to the moon and the stars.

He talked so much that he became very tired. Finally, just before the sun came up, he fell asleep. He was so tired that he was still sleeping when the sun rose. The other animals and the birds went to get their new names, but Coyote kept on sleeping. When Coyote woke up at last, it was just getting dark.

"Hah," Coyote said. "This is good. I am up before sunrise. I will certainly be the first one to get my name."

Coyote ran to the place where the Creator was still waiting.

"I've come for my new name," Coyote said.

"That is good," said the Creator.

"I will be ... Quoh Why-yah-mah. I will be White Eagle!"

"That name has been taken," said the Creator.

"Then ... I will be Twee-tash. I will be Grizzly Bear."

"That name has already been given," the Creator said.

"Mountain Lion? Hawk? Wolf? Wolverine? Gray Squirrel? Chipmunk?" Coyote kept asking, but all of those names were taken.

"What names are left?" Coyote finally asked.

"Ah," said the Creator, "there is only one name left because no one else wanted it. That name is Speel-yi. Coyote. It is your name."

And it is still Coyote's name to this day.

Whether they are names we are given or names we earn, there will always be stories connected to every name. If we know the stories of our names, we can better know ourselves.

Migration Stories: More than any other contemporary people, Americans have been on the move for a long time. There are very, very few people who live, as I do, in the same house in which they were raised. It is said that most Americans move at least three times during their lives.

According to my family traditions, most of my ancestors, even some of the Native American ones, migrated to the United States. My Abenaki great-grandfather, Louis Bowman, was born in St. Francis, Quebec, where the Abenaki Indian Reserve of Odanak is still located. He came to the United States in the 1860s, enlisted in the army, fought on the side of the Union in the Civil War, and became a naturalized United States citizen. His wife, Alice Van Antwerp, came from a family that was Dutch and, apparently, Mohican Indian.

Another of my ancestors, whose name was Dunham, came over on the *Mayflower*. The ship records showed he died while at sea—before he was married and before he fathered any children. Then how did he get to be my ancestor? Well, it seems that two years later he turned up alive in the records at Plimouth Plantation, the *Mayflower* colony in Massachusetts. His story is that he feigned his own death on board the ship so that he could escape from people in England who wished to do him harm.

On my father's side of the family, both my grandmother and grandfather came from the town of Trnava in Slovakia. Their family names were Hrdlika and Bruchac. It was just before World War I, and my grandfather knew that a war was about to happen. Czechoslovakia was part of the Austro-Hungarian Empire then, and he did not want to be forced to be a soldier. He would not have been allowed to emigrate from Czechoslovakia, but he was allowed to travel to Austria.

When he got to Austria, he was able to leave for America with new papers that listed him not as Slovak but as Austrian. My grandmother, who was a cook, followed him later to America, where they would be married.

How did your grandparents or your great-grandparents or the first immigrants in your family come to America? There are many interesting stories there. Why not ask and find out?

Family Trees

Here is a family tree. An artist made it from my sketch and marked where you could put the names of your own relatives. You can trace this onto a piece of paper and fill it in yourself. Ask your parents, your aunts and uncles, and your

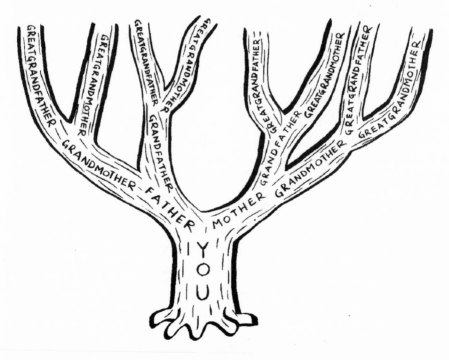

grandparents for the names you need. And ask them what stories they remember, too.

"When I Was Your Age..." Has anyone ever said that to you? If so, why not ask whoever said it to tell you what it was like when he or she was your age? It may be hard imagining your grandparents being your age, but they were and they have memories they can tell you about. Even your mother and father have stories that may surprise you, because with the passage of time comes change, and your life is sure to be different from theirs.

For instance, when I was growing up we did not get our first television until I was in fourth grade. That television was not like the ones we have today. It was a very large wooden box that had a small window in it, only eight inches across. It was very small, but the idea of having moving pictures inside a box was still very exciting. However, the picture on that television was in black and white. It would be many years before almost everyone would have color televisions in their homes.

My sons love to hear the story of how my grandfather and I got our first "color" television when I was in high school. By then we had heard about color television even though we had never seen it. One day a salesman came to our door.

"How would you like to have a color television?" he said. "I can sell you a converter that is *guar-an-teed* to turn your set into a color TV."

"How much does it cost?" my grandfather said.

"Ten dollars," said the salesman.

"Don't know if I can afford that," my grandfather said.

The salesman smiled. "For you, a special price—five dollars."

"It's a deal."

The salesman went out to his car and came back with a big briefcase. He opened it up and took out a piece of plastic that he taped over our screen. The bottom third of that plastic was tinged brown, the middle of it was green, and the top was blue. "There you go. Just wait ten minutes before you turn her on."

He took the five dollars from my grandfather and was out the door.

Ten minutes later we turned on our new color TV. The picture was no longer black and white. It was brown on the bottom, where the ground was; green in the middle, like the trees; and blue on top, like the sky. At first, since the show we were watching was about the outdoors, we thought that was just fine. Then *The Milton Berle Show* came on. When Milton Berle appeared on the screen, his chest was brown, his face was green, and his hair was blue. That was our color television, except it was the same colors all along. And that salesman was long gone.

Just as that experience of my first color television became a tale that I still love to relate, the things that happen to you today may be the stories you will tell when you get older.

History

As you may already know, a family's history is always linked to the larger histories of peoples and places and times. When you begin learning family stories about the past, you will probably want to know more about the times when and places where those stories happened.

I've found that oral history, history told in the form of a spoken story, can be very exciting. Telling history can be done in more than one way. Many storytellers earn their living by studying the lives of one or two real people who lived in the past. They find out everything they can about how those people dressed, how he or she talked, what kind of clothes the person wore, as well as the events in that person's life. Then they do storytelling programs in which they become that person. One of the first people to do this was an actor named Hal Holbrook, who presented a program called *Mark Twain Tonight* in which he played the part of writer Mark Twain, taking on his character or persona, sitting for hours in front of an audience telling Mark Twain's stories.

My sister Margaret, who is ten years younger than I am, is interested in both the English and the Abenaki histories of our family. She has made a careful study of medieval culture and belongs to the Society for Creative Anachronism. Her special interest is in women warriors, and her persona in the society is a woman leather merchant who also disguises herself as a male knight and fights in battles. She is very knowledgeable about the history of women who have disguised themselves as men and fought in wars—from the medieval past to World War II! Margaret has a great interest in an Abenaki woman named Molly Occutt, who was a healer and midwife in the mid-1700s. She tells stories about

Molly and has been doing the necessary research, both interviewing Abenaki elders and visiting libraries and museum archives, to dress as Molly did and tell her stories in the first person.

In one of the stories told about her, early one Monday Molly Occutt brought a basket of blueberries to the wife of a Methodist minister in the town of Bethel, Vermont. Instead of thanking Molly for her gift, the minister's wife assumed that Molly had picked the berries on Sunday—a day when people were not supposed to work—and so she scolded Molly for breaking the Sabbath. Although Molly was insulted by this ungrateful behavior, she left without saying a word. Several weeks later, though, Molly came back to visit the minister's wife. "I was right to pick those berries on Sunday," she said. "It was a beautiful day and I was happy that the Great Spirit had provided those berries for me."

Just imagine you are some person from the past. Abraham Lincoln or Elvis Presley. Sojourner Truth or Billie Holiday. What stories might you tell? Getting to know people—such as Sacagawea or Anne Frank—who lived long ago is a way to understand the past. Remember, the more you know, the better the stories will be. And your local library is one of the best places to seek out people of the past.

How can you remember family stories, stories about history, and other stories you've heard? Your memory can hold more things than you might believe. But you can also write things down to help you remember them.

Sometimes I keep a journal. I write down and keep a record of stories that people tell me. I don't always have to write down the whole story. Often only a few words or sentences are enough to help me remember a long story. I write down the month, day, and year at the start of each entry. I also write down who told me the story and where I was when I heard it. I use a whole page for each new story I hear, even though I might not fill up that page with what I first write. Sometimes I turn back to that page later on when I have time—perhaps in the evening just before I go to bed—and add things I forgot to write down the first time.

Here's a sample from one of my journals that I kept while I was a volunteer teacher in Ghana, West Africa.

Wednesday, June 26, 1967 *Today Nelson Amegashie, one of my students, told me about Yiyi the Spider. Yiyi is the favorite trickster figure in the stories of the Anlo people. But Yiyi sometimes outwits himself.*

One year there is a great famine. Everyone goes out looking for food. As Yiyi walks along, he comes upon a stone with eyes. But he is so tired that he says nothing. He just sits down under a tree near the stone. An antelope comes along and sees the stone.

"It is a stone with eyes!" the antelope says. Then it falls down dead.

Interesting, *Yiyi thinks. He drags the antelope home for dinner. Next day he goes back by the stone. A rabbit comes by.*

"What is that?" says Yiyi, pointing at the stone.

"It is a stone with eyes," says the rabbit.

The rabbit falls down dead, too. Yiyi drags it home. From then on, every day, Yiyi goes out and sits by that stone.

One day, though, a squirrel is up in that tree. It sees what Yiyi is doing. It comes down the tree and walks by Yiyi.

"What is that?" says Yiyi, pointing at the stone.

"What is what?" says the squirrel.

"That there," says Yiyi.

"I don't see anything," says the squirrel.

"Are you blind?" says Yiyi, getting angry. "That!"

"What?" says the squirrel.

Yiyi says. "Can't you see? It is a stone with eyes."

Then Yiyi falls down dead.

As interesting as that story was, I am not sure I could have remembered it almost thirty years later without having written it down. But whenever I read that journal entry, I can hear Nelson Amegashie's voice and remember other things that happened that day in Ghana. Keeping your own journal will help you hold on to ideas that you might otherwise forget.

Ask the Land: Stories of Place

Maps are wonderful things. You have heard tales about treasure maps that lead to buried riches. Treasure maps make us all think of magic and mystery. But every map has mysteries and magic hidden in the names of states and counties, cities and towns, mountains and rivers and lakes. Those names are the echoes of many strong memories held between earth and sky.

What is the name of the city or town where you live? What county is it located in? What is the name of your state, of the bodies of water close to your home? Those names all have stories connected to them. They can lead you to colorful people, to interesting histories, and to wonderful tales of the near and far past. You can find many stories by just asking the land. Here are a few of the stories of place from my own map.

I live in the small town of Greenfield Center, New York. Greenfield Center, which is located in the Adirondack Mountains foothills of northern New York State, gets its name, some say, from the Greenfield family. In the 1800s Abner Greenfield and his son Bill Greenfield became well-known as woodsmen and storytellers. Bill, it is said, was the world's greatest liar. By that it is meant he was the best at telling tall tales. "Tall tales" mean that these stories are a real stretch! When you tell a tall tale, you don't really intend to deceive anyone, just to have fun and exercise your imagination by exaggerating the truth. There's even a group of storytellers from my region called the Adirondack Liars' Club. I'm a charter member. What we do is sit around and tell each other tales, tall tales. Here's one of the tales about Bill Greenfield that I've told at meetings of our club. You will have to decide for yourself what parts of it are absolutely real and what parts are not.

BILL GREENFIELD AND THE COLD DAY
North America/Northeast/Adirondack

One cold winter day, Bill Greenfield and his father, Abner, decided to go out for a walk. It was so cold that day that you had to pound the air to breathe it, but the Greenfields were tough and didn't intend to allow a little chill to keep them inside. They didn't think it could ever be too cold for them to go out for a walk.

They walked along until they saw some birds on a tree branch. But those birds were not moving. When Bill and his father got close enough, they saw those birds were frozen solid. They could see little frozen songs coming out of their open mouths.

They walked on a little farther until they came to a clearing, and in that clearing they saw a rabbit. It was all crouched down and it looked scared, but it didn't move because it was frozen solid, too. Bill looked around to see what had scared that rabbit. There, frozen in midair, was a fox that had just been about to jump on it. Bill, who was kind of soft-hearted, felt sorry for the rabbit, so he took that fox and turned it around in midair so that when spring came and the two animals thawed out, the fox would miss that rabbit and it'd have a chance to get away.

It was so cold that Bill and his father saw they would have to do something to get themselves warmed up. So they gathered some wood and tried to make themselves a fire. But every time Bill lit a match, the flame on that match would freeze solid. Bill was not a man to waste anything, though. So every time one of those matches froze, he just broke off the flame and dropped it in an empty tobacco tin he had with him. For years after that, any time Bill wanted to make a fire, all he had to do was thaw out one of those little frozen flames.

Well, they saw it was too cold for them to stay out any

longer. They started for home. Bill had forgotten to wear his heavy boots and his feet were getting cold. His feet got so cold that they froze solid. As soon as Bill and his father walked in the door, Abner called out to his wife to bring them a pot of water to thaw out Bill's feet. Now, when you have frostbite, you should thaw out your feet in *cold* water. That's the truth. But Bill's ma, she didn't understand what they wanted. She brought out a pot of boiling water. Bill put his feet right into that water! And his feet were so cold that six inches of ice formed on top of the water as soon as he put his feet in. Luckily, Bill's feet thawed out and he was just fine. But from then on, Bill and his father knew that there really were some times when it was just a little too cold for them to go out for a walk.

Tall tales, like the one I've just told about Bill Greenfield, are very much a part of the American folk tradition. They may be based on a real person whose exploits are exaggerated or on someone who was totally imaginary. You may be familiar with such characters as Paul Bunyan or Johnny Appleseed or Pecos Bill, but there are many other heroes—and heroines, too—of the tall tales of the United States. Johnny Darling, Joe Magarak, the Swamp Angel, and High John the Conqueror are only a few of the lesser-known but equally fascinating people to be found in tall tales. Even though tall tales are often wild and exaggerated stories, they contain a great deal of truth. Not only can they make us laugh, they can also point out things that we need to know about being quick-witted or brave, about overcoming adversity. Tall tales remind us that real stories may not be true and true stories may not be real.

Saratoga County, where I live, gets its name, according to popular legend, from the mineral springs that flow here. Some say that Saratoga is really Saragh-tau-kah, or a variant spelling, and that it is a Mohawk Indian word meaning "place of many springs." However, like many names thought to be Indian, the popular understanding of Saratoga's meaning may be wrong. I have a Mohawk friend named Daniel Thompson who says the name really comes from a Mohawk word that means "sore heel." Perhaps the person who had that wounded heel soaked it in the healing waters of the High Rock Spring.

That spring, called the Medicine Spring of the Great Spirit by the Mohawk people, flows freely in a little valley near the center of the present-day city of Saratoga Springs. Now we know it as the High Rock Spring because the iron in its water has built up a tall red mineral cone. The area around the spring was once a swamp, so those who visited the spring had to place great logs down to walk on them across the soft earth. The spring's water was regarded by the Mohawk people as a special medicine, which could heal all kinds of ailments.

A hundred years ago, when the city of Saratoga did some work around that spring, they dug up those logs that had been used to bridge the swamp. Under those logs was yet another layer of logs, and another layer below that. There were so many layers of logs laid down that it was clear people had been coming to that spring for many hundreds of years.

The healing power of this place was said to be a gift from the Creator. No warfare or quarreling of any kind was allowed in the area around the spring. So, for many years, the Medicine Spring of the Great Spirit was a place of peace. To be healed, however, a person's mind had to be free from anger or thoughts of war.

There is the story of the first white man to see the spring, Sir William Johnson, a special friend of the Mohawk people. In the 1760s the Mohawk people carried him to the spring in the hope it would help to heal his gout. But Sir William Johnson was not able to stay here long enough for the waters to heal him. He was called away to a war council. Sir William Johnson never regained his health and died only a few years later. And it is thought even today, just as the legend said, that those matters of war prevented him from being healed by the medicine spring.

The mountain range that crosses upper New York State is called the Adirondacks. The name Adirondack was first used to refer to one of the nations of Abenaki-speaking people who lived in the region. *Adirondack* comes from the Mohawk word *ratiron,* which means "porcupine" or "eater of bark." My Abenaki ancestors told this story, which explains how the mountains came to be called the Adirondacks.

HOW THE ADIRONDACKS GOT THEIR NAME
North America/Northeast/Abenaki

Throughout the generations, the Iroquois, who lived to the south of the mountains, and the Abenaki people, who lived farther to the north and the east, were sometimes at odds with each other. But both the Iroquois and the Abenakis hunted often in those mountains.

One day two groups of young men—one a party of Iroquois, the other a party of Abenakis—met each other by accident at a place near Middle Saranac Lake where the water is narrow. The Iroquois stood on the west bank and the Abenakis stood on the east bank.

"You are hunting in our territory," the Iroquois called over to them.

"No," answered the Abenakis, "you are in our territory."

"You must leave," the Iroquois shouted back.

"No," the Abenakis called back to them, "you must leave."

"We will cross over and make you leave," the Iroquois shouted.

"No, we will cross over and make you leave," the Abenakis answered.

But neither the Iroquois nor the Abenakis crossed the water. If either did so, it would probably start a big fight. Neither side really wanted to fight with the other, but neither side wanted to give in. The two parties of young men stood there facing each other like two wildcats on opposite sides of a fallen log. Finally, the Abenakis became hungry and started peeling bark off the pine trees to eat. The pithy inner bark of the white pine is very nutritious.

"You are Adirondacks," said the Iroquois. "You are porcupines! You are eaters-of-bark."

"Hah," said the Abenakis, "we may be porcupines, but you are Maguak. You are people-who-are-afraid."

"Adirondack," the Iroquois shouted.

"Maguak," the Abenakis answered.

Then the young men in both parties began to laugh. They decided that they had each gotten the better of the other. The Iroquois turned and went south while the Abenakis turned and went north.

So, to this day the Iroquois are called Maguak in the Abenaki language, while the Abenaki people and that region where they always hunted became known as the Adirondacks.

There are silent stories all around, and the Adirondack region is no exception. The mountains and hills were covered with trees, which were the basis for the timber industry in the eighteenth and nineteenth centuries. Every river and stream in the Adirondacks has its own tales to tell about when logs were floated down each spring in great log drives. The folklore of the region is also full of songs and stories from that time of logging. I grew up hearing ballads sung about those log drives, when brave men rode the logs down wild rivers to Glens Falls, where the pine and spruce and fir was milled into lumber.

When the logs got stuck on the riverbanks or the rocks in the river, they would pile up into a great logjam. Some logjams were three stories high and had more than ten thousand logs caught in them. The most dangerous and best-paying jobs were those of the men who broke up the logjams. The crews that broke up the jams often consisted of a boatman and two other men who would jump out onto the jam to pry loose the logs with a hooked pole called a peavey.

Have you ever known someone who bragged about doing something but didn't really know how to do it? Here is an Adirondack ballad that tells the story of a man who bragged about his ability to "run the boat."

THE BALLAD OF JOE THOMAS

North America/Northeast/Adirondack

He said he'd been a boatman for fifteen years and more.
He'd run the Hudson River where the thunderin' torrents
    pour.
He dreaded nor feared no danger while in his own canoe.
He'd run the Hudson River and the Indian River, too.

'Twas on a Sunday morning, just at the hour of ten,
Joe Thomas and his boat crew their business did begin.
He rammed his boat into the jam, and split her bow in
    two,
And soon she filled with water and washed away his crew.

He'd bothered the foreman all spring to let him run the
    boat,
But I guess he got his fill of her when from him she did
    float.
For his boat lies on the bottom and her rigging is cast
    away,
And Joe's breaking jams along the bank for a dollar and a
    half a day.

Lots of songs tell stories. A storytelling song is usually called a ballad, and ballads are found all over the world. Very often they deal with the lives and tragedies of working people. Ballads are not just part of the past; they are still being written. Many popular songs are actually ballads. Country-western music and folk music are filled with examples of this. Woody Guthrie in the 1930s, Bob Dylan in the 1960s, Joni Mitchell in the 1970s, and Bruce Springsteen now are a few twentieth-century American musicians whose songs include many ballads. In the nineteenth century, one of the most popular ballads was "The Ballad of Jesse James," which tells the story of the famous American outlaw. Another popular nineteenth-century ballad, which tells of the tragic death of a young cowboy, is known as "The Streets of Laredo" or "The Cowboy's Lament." "John Henry," the tale of an African American steel driver who beats a steam engine, and "Casey Jones," the sad story of a brave railroad engineer, are two more examples of American ballads that remain popular to this day.

New York is named after a region of England called York. When the English colonists sought a name for their settlement in what they called the New World, they named it New York, in part because it reminded them of that green part of England. Other states have Native American names. Connecticut means "the long river" in Abenaki. Wisconsin means "everything is good" in Menominee. Vermont, on the other hand, comes from the French words *vert*, meaning "green," and *mont*, meaning "mountain"; it really is the Green Mountain State. Every state's name spins its own story.

———

Now follow your own treasure map. See what stories or traditions you already know about your town or city, your county, your region, and your state. If you don't know any, try asking a parent or a teacher, or visit the library. By listening to the land and finding out about where you live, you will begin to uncover your own treasure trove of stories—stories that will always be yours.

ACTIVITIES

O Sit alone in a quiet room and listen to all the things around you. Imagine all the stories relating to the noises. Examples: The birds—Imagine a bird flying to gather twigs to make a nest. A car—Imagine where the person driving the car may be going for the day.

O When sitting with a friend, clear your mind and truly listen to what your friend is saying. Try to see what your friend sees, and put yourself in his or her shoes. Pay attention to how your friend says what she or he wants to express.

O Sit in a quiet room and listen to a song for just the words; then listen closely just to the music. Consider how each way of listening makes you feel.

O Sit at a family gathering and ask each person to tell you his or her recollection of a past event. Compare how their stories are the same or different.

O Sit in a quiet room and listen to yourself read a story aloud.

O Sit with a group of friends and have them all talk about different subjects. See which stories have particular personal meaning for you; think about why these stories resonate for you.

2

We look, but we don't always see. Although we have been given two eyes so that we can see the world in depth, we often see only the surface. Instead of seeing the world all around us, we may only look at what is right in front of us. Day after day we have the same routines and we no longer pay attention to the subtle changes that are always happening. We no longer see the faces of the people we pass or the changing of the seasons. Sometimes we hardly see anything at all.

One autumn I was waiting for a train at a station just north of New York City. The parking lot was on the other side of the tracks, and passengers had to walk across them to get to the platform. As I stood there, a man wearing a suit and carrying a briefcase started from the parking lot toward the tracks. When I saw him, I became worried. I could see a fast train coming from around the corner, a train that would not stop at that station. The man was wearing headphones and listening to loud classical music on his tape player. He was looking straight ahead, not seeing anything but the platform ahead of him on the other side of the tracks. Just before he stepped in front of the train, which he didn't see coming, a railroad worker grabbed his shoulder and pulled him back. The train went by him so close that his hat blew off. Looking but not seeing had almost cost him his life.

Observing, really seeing, is another way to discover stories. Here is a simple exercise you can do with a friend to find out how well you see. Close your eyes and try to picture the room in which you are sitting with your friend. Now, without opening your eyes, have your friend ask you questions about the things you could have seen. If the room has windows, your friend could ask you how many windows are in the room and what can be seen just outside those windows. Or your friend could ask you to describe the clothes he or she is wearing or even ask you such things as what color his or her eyes are. The questions should not be difficult, just questions about the things that you should have been able to see easily if you were really observing. Close Your Eyes and See can also be played as a game with two or more people. By repeating this exercise again and again, anyone can strengthen the powers of observation.

Seeing, of course, is not just seeing the world around you. That is very necessary, but you also have to be able to see *into* things, to observe and understand. You have to see others and see yourself as others see you. Also, when you experience a story, you will understand it better if you can see it in your mind.

As Others See Us:
Stories as a Way of Understanding

Those who cannot see beyond the surface are often fooled. One of the oldest stories about being fooled by not seeing deeply is the Aesop's fable of the fox and the grapes. Aesop was a storyteller in ancient Greece. His name meant "the Ethiopian," for Aesop had been brought as a slave from Africa, and the stories he told appear to have their roots in African traditions. There are many versions of this tale of the fox and the grapes told all over the world. In one version the fox tries to jump up and grab a bunch of grapes hanging from a high branch. But it cannot jump high enough. "Those grapes are probably not good," the fox finally says. "Those grapes are probably sour." In another version of the story, a hungry fox sees what it thinks are grapes that have fallen into a pond. It can see them just below the surface of the water. The fox jumps in to get them but cannot find them. Every time the fox jumps in, the grapes seem to disappear. The fox keeps trying, but it only gets wetter. The grapes are actually hanging from a vine in a tree over the water. All that the fox saw was the reflection of the grapes on the pond's still surface.

If we do not look at things with understanding, we cannot really see other people—we only see a reflection of ourselves. The Jewish tradition is full of stories about seemingly powerful people who fail to observe and understand. Because of their blindness, they are defeated when the supposedly weaker person is better at seeing how things really are.

Here is a story from Russia about one such self-centered person.

Can You Pluck My Rooster?

Eastern Europe/Russia/Yiddish

Long ago, in Russia, there was a wealthy landlord. He was a good man, but his steward was not. His steward was a very proud and vain man. The steward treated the landlord's tenants very unfairly, especially those who were Jews. He thought that all peasants were fools.

One winter day the landlord and his steward were driving around the estate in a sleigh when they saw one of the Jewish tenants working in his field. He was barefoot and his clothes were torn, but the landlord immediately stopped the sleigh and spoke to the man.

"Levi," the landlord said with a smile, "how can you work when it is so cold? Isn't seven better than five?"

Levi stopped working and came over to the sleigh. "Lordship," Levi said, "that is true. But thirty-two is still more than seven and five."

When Levi said that, the landlord began to laugh. The steward, though, was puzzled. He could not see what they were talking about.

"Levi," the landlord continued, "has your house burned down lately?"

"Lordship," Levi replied, "it has burned down twice, and this spring it will burn down a third time."

Once again the landlord laughed and once again the steward, who thought all peasants were stupid, was confused.

"Master," said the steward, "we have other things to do than talk with this foolish man."

The landlord looked at his steward and then gestured for Levi to come close to the sleigh. He put his hand on Levi's arm.

"Tell me, my friend," the landlord said to Levi, "can you pluck my rooster in three handfuls?"

"Lordship," said Levi, laughing as he spoke, "I am sure I can do it in two."

As they drove along, the steward was silent until the landlord turned to him.

"Now you tell me," the landlord said, "what my clever friend Levi and I were talking about."

"Master," said the steward, "I'm sure that there are better things to do than talk with such an ignorant man."

"You mean you could not understand anything we said?"

"Master," said the steward, "if you think I'm not able to understand the words of a simple peasant, then why am I your steward?"

"You are my steward," said the landlord, "because I've found no one better to take your place. Now, to prove you are worthy to remain in that position, answer this question. Tell me, what did it mean when we spoke of five and seven and thirty-two?"

"My lord," said the steward, "give me some time to think of this."

"You have one week. Then you must tell me the answer."

The steward thought and thought, but he could not solve the problem. Finally, at the end of the week, he went to Levi's house.

"Levi," the steward said, "what did you and my master mean with your talk of five and seven and thirty-two?"

"Nothing difficult," said Levi. "Surely an intelligent man such as you sees the answer."

"I will pay you five rubles to tell me," said the steward.

"Surely, anything I could tell you is not worth that much," said Levi. "Do you not have better things to do than talk with such an ignorant man as me?"

"Ten rubles then," said the steward.

"What can I tell you that you do not already know?" asked Levi.

"I have the power to throw you out of your house," said the steward.

"You may do as you please, lordship," said Levi.

But he did not answer the question. The steward kept offering him more and more rubles, but still Levi did not give him the answer.

Finally the steward named a very large sum of money. "That is half of all I own," he said.

"Ah," said Levi, "you really do need to know. Then I accept your offer. Here is the answer. When the noble land-lord spoke of seven being better than five, he meant that it is easier to work outside in the seven months when there is no snow than in the five months of winter. I told him that thirty-two was greater because we all have thirty-two teeth and we must still eat, whatever the season may be."

When the steward went to the landlord and told him the answer, the landlord was pleased. "Good," he said. "You are right. Now tell me what we meant when we talked about Levi's house burning down."

"Let me think about that," said the steward.

"You have seven days," said the landlord.

Once again the steward could not see the answer. So he went again to Levi. Just as before, Levi was not eager to tell him. The steward offered him more and more money, but Levi still refused. Finally the steward offered him the same amount he had offered before.

"If what you offered me before was half of all you own, does this mean that you are offering me all the rubles you have left?"

"Yes," said the steward, gritting his teeth.

"Then I accept your offer. The answer is very simple. It is said among my people that providing for a daughter's marriage costs as much as having your house burn down. My wife and I have three daughters. Two are already married and one will be married in the spring."

The steward gave the peasant the last of his money and returned to the landlord. When the landlord heard the second answer, he nodded with pleasure.

"You have done well," he said. "Now you must tell me the meaning of the third thing of which we spoke. Tell me why Levi laughed so heartily when he said he could pluck my rooster in only two handfuls."

The steward went back to the peasant.

"I have no money left," the steward said, "but I beg you

to tell me the answer. Why did you laugh when you said you could pluck his rooster in only two handfuls?"

"I would rather not answer that question," said Levi. "In fact, I do not think you want to know."

"By the bones of Saint Peter," said the steward, "I must know. I am now a penniless man and will lose my job as steward and starve unless you tell me the answer."

"Let us make a bargain," said Levi. "I will give you your answer *and* your money back if you will give me one thing."

"Name it," said the steward, "and it will be yours."

"Give me your job as steward."

The steward paused and then shook his head. "By the names of all the saints in heaven," he said, "there is nothing else I can do. The job is yours; now tell me the answer."

"Ah," said Levi, "it is plain as the nose on your face. You are the rooster, and I stripped you of all you owned with only two questions."

The steward hung his head in shame. He began to leave, but Levi called him back.

"Here," Levi said, giving the man back his money, "take your rubles and leave this land in peace."

The former steward did just that. From that day on Levi was the steward. The landlord was well pleased, and all agreed that the former peasant was the finest and the fairest steward they had ever known.

This story is more than two hundred years old, but its truth is as important today as it was in the century when it was first told. A person who cannot see the wisdom in others often turns out to be the one who is a fool.

Try seeing this story from the point of view of each of the three characters in it. Pretend that you are Levi or the wealthy landlord or the mean-spirited steward. Tell the story as if you were one of those three talking about something that had happened to you. Now try a second character and tell the story from his viewpoint. Think about how the story is different each time. There are many ways of seeing, and often a new way of seeing gives us a new way of understanding.

Rites of Passage: Stories about Growth and Change

Sometimes, as a result of seeing things in a new way, we are able to change our lives. As a young person, you are growing and changing every day. But when do you go from being a boy to being a man, from being a girl to being a woman? Is it a moment, a certain age, an experience that causes change?

In the past virtually every culture had its own unique and clearly defined rites of passage. At a certain time in the life of a young person, elders in the community would decide that person was ready to move into adulthood. By completing some well-defined task, the young person would pass through childhood into adult life. Today there are very few clearly defined rites of passage in America for young people.

Good examples of rites of passage still exist, however. In the Jewish American community, there is still the ceremony of the bar mitzvah for boys moving into manhood and, increasingly, the bat mitzvah for girls moving into womanhood. In the Native American community, it was common for a young man or a young woman to go on a vision quest when they were ready to become an adult. Adolescents would be taken out alone into the woods or onto the plain or up on a mountain, far from other people. They would be told by their elders what to do and how to act. Then they would sit in one place for several days without eating. They were supposed to listen and watch. Their job was to pray for a vision that would help them for the rest of their lives.

Seeking a vision is not just something done by Native Americans; it is a practice found throughout the world in many cultures, including the Judeo-Christian tradition. In the New Testament, Jesus Christ goes out into the wilderness for forty days. When he returns, after hearing the word of God, he is ready to take on the work of spreading his message of peace.

It's been said that one reason gangs are so popular is because they offer young people a way to grow and change, to go through a rite of passage. But the traditional purpose of a rite of passage is not to make young people violent and dangerous. Instead, it is to help them become useful, happy, and self-confident members of their culture. A rite of passage is an outward recognition of the changes that have gone on within a child who is becoming an adult. It is a way to symbolize and celebrate that growth.

THE HERO'S JOURNEY

Not all of us have the help and understanding or guidance to sustain us through a vision quest. But all of us can listen to stories about rites of passage. By hearing a story, we can envision ourselves on that same journey. Joseph Campbell, a famous author who writes about myths and legends, called this part of life the hero's journey. In that journey, which is like a circle, a young man or woman leaves home to seek his or her fortune. Along the way, obstacles arise. The hero or heroine must overcome those obstacles to continue. He or she learns from the experience and then continues on. Eventually the hero or heroine returns home, strengthened by the experience and ready to help his or her family and people. Most stories about heroes or heroines have these four parts:

○ *Departure*—The hero or heroine leaves home.

○ *Difficulty*—The hero or heroine faces great obstacles. The hardships include evil people, threats by monsters, and abandonment.

○ *Discovery*—The hero or heroine finds a way to overcome the obstacles. Doing this, he or she gains power or is given a special gift.

○ *Return*—The hero or heroine goes back home, often using what he or she has gained (which may be material wealth or knowledge) to help the people.

Think of stories that you know, perhaps even a story from the newspaper, the movies, or television. Do any of those stories fit that four-part structure? In all parts of the world there are many such stories. In the British Isles there are the tales of a young boy named Jack who must defeat one or more giants. The Jack stories came to America with the British settlers and are still told all over the American South. In

Native American traditions, the hero is often a boy dressed in ragged clothing whose parents have died. However, because this young man has always listened to the old stories and watched everything around him, he is the one who is able to defeat a monster that threatens his people. In some of the stories, when that little boy returns to his village after defeating the monster, he has grown up overnight and is a tall, strong man wearing new, beautiful clothing. When you start to look for hero stories, you'll see them in everything from King Arthur to *Star Wars* and *The Lion King*.

There are just as many such stories about girls. Cinderella is the story of a poor but honest girl who finds success. Cinderella stories are found all over the world, from Europe to China to the Americas. Some of these stories end with the heroine being rescued or marrying a prince, but that is not always the case. There are also stories of independent women and of women who are the ones who do the rescuing. The French story of Joan of Arc, the little peasant girl who sees a vision from God and goes on to lead the armies of France to victory in battle, is one such powerful legend that is based on history.

In the traditions of India, there are many tales of heroes and heroines. Here is one in which a princess overcomes great difficulties.

THE WISDOM OF PRINCESS MAYA
Asia/India/Hindu

Long ago there was a beautiful princess named Maya. Unlike some of the other girls, she was not interested in fine clothing and jewels and talking about the things that happened in the palace. She was interested in learning. Because of that, she was sent to study with wise scholars. When she returned she had learned many things. She had learned that whatever people do, they will get what they deserve. She had learned that wise people do not question what fate has brought to them. Instead, one must always watch and listen in order to understand. Knowing this, even the simplest things can bring great happiness. As a result of these teachings, Princess Maya understood many things. She even understood the language of the animals.

Her father, the king, however, was not pleased with her. Instead of bowing low to him in the morning, she would simply smile at him and say, "Good morning, Father. May you get all that you deserve."

"What is wrong with my daughter?" the king said to his chief councillor. "I do not like the way she speaks to me."

"Perhaps it is time for her to be married, sire," said the councillor, who was a very wise man.

"How can I do this?" said the king. "Anyone who marries a princess would expect to get a large dowry. I have no money to give away."

"A poor man makes a better husband than no man at all," said the councillor.

The king was not sure that he understood what the councillor had said, but he called Princess Maya to him.

"Daughter," he said, "it is time for you to be married."

"As you wish, Father," said Princess Maya.

"Then I will offer you to the first stranger I see tomorrow

morning," said the king. "That is all that you deserve! And when you are married, you must leave my kingdom with your husband."

The king expected Princess Maya to beg him to change his mind. But she did not question what fate had brought to her. She had seen a tall, thin stranger with a beggar's bowl enter the courtyard just as darkness settled over the palace. She knew that man would be the first stranger her father would see the next morning. She had looked closely at that man and had seen there was more to him than might be seen at first glance. Although he was a beggar, he was gentle and kind. So she simply smiled at the king and said, "As you wish, Father."

The next morning, as the king looked out his window, he saw a tall, lean stranger in the courtyard below. The man was poorly dressed and carried a beggar's bowl.

"You," called out the king, "do you have a wife?"

"No," said the man. "I am too poor to have a wife."

"Not any longer," said the king. "You can have my daughter. Go see my councillor and he will take care of it."

The king was so angry at his daughter that he didn't go to the wedding. Later that evening he called his councillor to him.

"Is my daughter married?" he asked.

"Yes, sire. She left with her new husband. She seemed quite happy and said that she has what she deserves."

"Did the man demand a dowry?"

"No, sire. He said that Princess Maya is all that he wants."

Although Princess Maya's husband appeared to be a beggar, she knew there was more to him than that. Although he was poor, he carried himself like a prince. He spoke gently to everyone and was not angry or bitter. He treated Princess Maya with great kindness and courtesy as they traveled together. What little he had, he shared with her equally.

One evening as they sat together, her husband told her his story.

"I was not born a beggar," he said. "I became one out of shame. One day I went out hunting with my servants. I grew tired and lay down by a termite mound to sleep. When I woke I was hungry. I ate and ate, but my hunger was never satisfied. No matter how much I ate, I still grew thinner and thinner. In shame I left my family and became a beggar."

Princess Maya listened carefully to her husband's story.

"Where is that termite mound?" she asked.

"It is near the forest by the lake," he said. "We will camp in that same place tomorrow night."

The following day, the two of them set out. When they reached the termite mound, it was still afternoon.

"My husband," said Princess Maya, "you look tired. Lie down and sleep while I go into the town to get some food."

Her husband did as she said. Then, instead of going into town, Princess Maya hid herself behind a mango tree. Soon her husband fell asleep with his face turned toward the termite mound and his mouth open. As Princess Maya watched, something began to crawl out of his mouth. It was a huge snake. Another snake, exactly like the first, came crawling out of the termite mound.

The two snakes reared up and faced each other. Because Princess Maya had learned the language of animals, she could understand what they said.

"You lazy one," said the snake from the termite mound. "Can't you go and find your own food? Instead you live in that young prince's stomach and eat all that he puts into his mouth."

"You are the lazy one," said the snake that had crawled out of the mouth of Princess Maya's husband. "All that you do all day is sleep inside that termite hill on top of a mound of gold and jewels."

"I am sorry no one has realized that the way to kill you is to put a cupful of black mustard seeds into that young man's mouth," said the first snake.

"And I am sorry," said the second snake, "that no one knows that the way to kill you is by pouring a bucket of hot vinegar into that termite mound."

Then the first snake crawled back into the mouth of Princess Maya's husband while the second snake crawled back into the termite mound.

Princess Maya did not hesitate. She ran to the village market. There she used one of her bracelets to buy a cupful of black mustard seeds and a bucketful of vinegar. With the mustard seeds and the vinegar she killed the two snakes, curing her husband and winning a great treasure for the two of them.

Now that he was cured, her husband told her that he was, as his wife had always suspected, a prince. The two of them returned to his palace. There they lived long and well, ruling their kingdom together. So it was that Princess Maya saved her husband through her gift, the love of learning.

There are all kinds of heroes and heroines in stories—men, women, animals. And these stories remind us that heroes exist all around us, in story and in life. We will always find many stories of heroes—that is, if we take the time to look.

The Eye of the Heart: Stories about the Divine

Stories also have the power to take us deep within. They can take us to the world of the unknown and the imagined. Our everyday world is a temporal one—we are aware of the passage of time. But stories take us into a timeless place, a magical world where time no longer has meaning. One of the powers of story is to lead the listener or reader to discover new worlds. Stories of the divine always have to do with that which we cannot see with our everyday eyes. These are stories in which we can look within and find deeper meanings that inspire us. Every religion has such stories and such holy books; the Hebrew Talmud, the Ramayana and the Bhagavad Gita of India, the Christian Bible, and the Muslim Koran are filled with sacred stories that were related long ago. But there are new stories of the sacred being told every day. These stories, past and present, explain to people how the world came to be. Stories can remind us that there are forces beyond our human lives that support our morality and our social order. They help us cope with illness, disasters, and death. They provide us with deeply meaningful shared experiences.

In short, sacred stories help us to understand the mysteries of life. Without sacred stories, our lives and the things that happen to us may seem meaningless. We all have to cope with great problems. Illness, the deaths of people we love, problems it seems we cannot overcome are all part of our human condition. Faced by such things, we may think that nothing really matters and so it doesn't matter what we do. When we begin to feel that way, we need to hear sacred stories. Those stories remind us that other people have had similar problems and still found meaning in their lives. Sacred stories can help us to understand the divine.

The divine is that which proceeds from the sacred or is concerned with sacred things. The sacred is often defined as something very out of the ordinary related to spirituality or religious beliefs. Religion is usually described as a shared system of spiritual beliefs through which people see the world in a reverent way. All of this is connected to the belief in, as the *American Heritage Dictionary* defines *religion*, "a superhuman God who created the universe and all life in it."

The Lakota people express it more simply. They say we must never forget to see through the eye of the heart, *Cante ista*. Looking at things through the eye of the heart, though, means looking at all things with understanding. Hearing stories of the divine told from many different beliefs can help us remember the importance of tolerance. If we see through the eye of the heart, we see a world in which faith and the life of the spirit can survive.

In the early 1700s, a Quaker missionary met with a group of Native Americans on Long Island. He wanted to teach them about God. They listened carefully to what he said to them. Then he asked them a question.

"Brothers," he said, "do you also believe in God?"

"Yes," they said. Then one of the Indians smoothed the earth with his left hand, took a stick, and drew a circle. "This is Menitto," he said. "This is the Great Spirit."

"I do not understand," said the Quaker missionary. "Explain this to me."

"Menitto," the Indian man said, "is all eye. Menitto sees everything, even into our hearts. We cannot see Menitto, but we are always in the sight of the Great Spirit. His circle is all around us. All of us are within the circle of the eye of the Great Spirit."

The Quaker missionary nodded his head. "I see that circle," he said. "I understand."

Contemporary American culture is full of stories of the divine, quite apart from the sacred teachings to be found in the holy scriptures of different religions. These stories of everyday people sometimes are even turned into songs. Often they involve small, very personal miracles. I remember a song called "Scarlet Ribbons," which was popular when I was a child. In the story that the song is based upon, a little girl who is very ill asks her father for only one thing for Christmas: She wants a red ribbon for her hair. She asks him for this on Christmas Eve. Since the little girl's mother is dead, her father is the only person she has left. When he hurries out to try to buy her a scarlet ribbon, he finds that there are either none left in the stores or that the stores are already closed. He goes back home and falls asleep by her bedside, after praying to the Lord for guidance. When he wakes up the next morning, Christmas Day, he hears his daughter laughing. He looks up to see that her bed is covered with scarlet ribbons.

Because stories of the divine are often based on another way of seeing, they may not sound logical at first. Yet there is usually logical meaning within those stories. There may be symbolic meaning. The story of the scarlet ribbons in one way symbolizes how, in Christian belief, God is said to be aware of everyone and everything in a caring way. It also shows in another way how a father who tries to provide for his child can be rewarded for his actions. Such lessons go beyond any one religious tradition. They are as true for Muslims, Hindus, and Christians as they are for Buddhists, Mormons, and Jews.

We also need to take care when we tell stories from someone else's religion. We must respect the views of others, especially when they are not the same as our own. Because of ignorance or intolerance, some of the stories of the past have shown other religious traditions in a negative way. This does not mean that we have to abandon our own spiritual beliefs.

What is the religious background of your family? What stories did your ancestors tell? There is a long tradition of storytelling to be found in every religious community. Sometimes those stories may be very serious, sometimes there may be an element of humor, but all of them contain reverence for the divine.

Reverence is the key. Stories of the spirit help us understand the sacred as it exists in ourselves and in others. So, as we listen to sacred stories—from our own and other religious traditions—we learn through reverence and respect. In those stories we find understanding and the wisdom to see things beyond our everyday vision. Sacred stories may help us see through the heart of creation.

Whether you look outside or inside, at the world around you or into your heart, wherever you look you can discover stories. Keep your eyes open and keep looking. The stories that you see will deepen your vision.

ACTIVITIES

○ Look out the window or stand outdoors and see how many things you notice happening at the same time.

○ Sit and watch your relatives at a family gathering. See how animated people's faces are and how different stories or words affect their body language.

○ Sit with a friend and notice how he or she looks at you when you speak—does your friend hold your attention or not?

○ Read a story aloud to a friend (or to small children) and consider how your friend reacts to a certain part.

○ Look at people on the street, or in the window of a café, and try to imagine what they are thinking, or what they are experiencing.

○ Watch people pass by as you sit on a park bench, on your front steps, or in your yard, and make up stories about the lives those people might lead.

○ Choose a place in nature or in a city and imagine all the people who have lived there or passed through, from earliest times to the present. What might the lives of those people have been like?

○ Cut pictures out of magazines or newspapers and paste them together to create a book. Then leaf through the book and make up a story to go with the pictures.

3

REMEMBERING

If you don't remember the things you've seen and heard, it is as if those things never happened. Without memory, it would be very hard to live our lives. Fortunately, memory is like a faithful friend who is usually there by your side. Think of all the things that you have to remember each day. You remember your name and where you live; you remember how to find your way to the houses of your friends or to the mall; you remember where you put things so that you can find them when you need them; you remember (you hope!) all of the answers to the test that you are about to take. The only time we seem to remember memory is when we actually do forget. "Now where did I put my keys?" "What was the date when the Civil War started?"

Without memory, there would be no history. Memory is what allows us to study the past. It is important for us to study the past because we can learn from the failures and successes of people who lived before us. Imagine yourself lost in a forest. As you walk along, you come to two different paths. One will lead you into danger. The other will bring you back home. You have never been to this place before, but as you stand there you remember a story that was told to you about this very place. In that story the person took one of those paths and found his way home. If you remember the story well enough, you can find your way home, too.

Knowing the past can protect the future. And story is one of the best ways to make those memories of the past come alive. Memorizing names and dates can be boring and difficult. Remembering the stories associated with those names and dates, however, can be exciting and interesting. If names and dates are the bones of the past, stories are the flesh and the breath that make those dry bones come alive again.

People who have studied memory have discovered that the human mind seems to be able to hold more memories than can be counted. It appears that we never use more than 10 percent of the capacity of our brain. Your mind isn't like a drawer that can easily be filled up. Your mind is like a powerful computer with almost unlimited capacity. It is more that we *think* we can't remember than it is that we lack the ability to hold on to things in our mind. As with a computer, we just need to know how to access the right file. Storytelling is like a powerful password.

Norma J. Livo is a storyteller and author. In her book *Storytelling: Process and Practice,* coauthored with Sandra A. Reitz, she talks about something she calls "story memory." Information in our mind that we shape into the form of a story is much easier to remember. Because our brains have been constructed as they are, she explains, we human beings are inclined to have "story memory." In other words, if you want to remember something, remember it in the form of a story.

JOKES AS STORIES

One memory device is to think of the story like a joke. After all, most jokes are just very short stories that are intended to make people laugh! So let's take a minute to look at the structure of the joke. A joke can be divided into three parts: the setup, the development, and the punch line.

The Setup: The main character or characters and the setting of the joke are introduced. We are given the story's main elements.

A man was driving his brand-new sports car down the road. No one else was on the highway, and so he decided to see how fast the car could go. He pushed the accelerator all the way to the floor, and before he knew it that car was doing over 120 miles an hour. All of a sudden, something passed his car as if it were standing still. It was a chicken with three legs!

In the setup, we are given a mental picture. If it is done well, that picture and the events in the joke are so interesting that we want to hear more. The man, the fast car, and the chicken faster than the car are the main elements of this little story.

The Development: The rest of the information is now given to us that will prepare us for the story's conclusion.

The man had never seen anything like that before. He followed the chicken as best he could, even though it was getting farther and farther ahead. Suddenly it turned off onto a dirt road that led up to a farm. The man followed. When he reached the farmyard and stopped his car, he got another surprise. That farmyard was full of chickens and every one of them had three legs. He saw a farmer sitting up on the porch and decided to go up and ask him about those chickens. But before he could say a word to the farmer, the farmer said to him, "I bet you want to know about those three-legged chickens."

"That's right," said the man.

"Well," said the farmer, "my wife and my son and me, we love to eat chickens. The problem is that all three of us love drumsticks. Now, most chickens only have two legs, so we bred these chickens to have three. That way, whenever we have chicken, we can each have a drumstick."

This middle part of the story has given us all the remaining information we need to know to understand the story. It has also led up to the conclusion of the story, the punch line.

The Punch Line: A punch line has to be both logical and unexpected so that it hits you like a punch. Because it is so unexpected, a punch line makes you laugh.

"Well," said the man to the farmer, "that is really something. But tell me, how do those three-legged chickens taste?"

The farmer shook his head. "I don't rightly know. We've never been able to catch one."

If you have ever known anyone who can't tell a joke, it is probably because he or she either forgets one of the three elements of a good funny story or tells them in the wrong order. If you were to give the punch line at the start of this story, it wouldn't work. If you were to forget the punch line, the story wouldn't be funny at all. There would be no conclusion. The story would also not be as funny without the buildup of the middle part, in which things are developed. And if you didn't introduce the main elements in the story, then you wouldn't be able to understand it as well.

Aristotle, a Greek philosopher who lived more than two thousand years ago, said that a story consists of three elements. They are the beginning, the middle, and the end. All of these many years later, those are the same three parts of a well-told joke or story.

A Feather's Touch: Stories That Heal

Stories are useful in many ways. Not only do they entertain us and amuse us, they also have the power to heal. This is true of both funny stories and serious ones. When people are ill but able to laugh, that laughter lessens the pain. There have been studies showing that people who are sick get well more quickly when they can laugh. Laughter is a great cure for depression. If you either hear a story that amuses you or turn the thing that made you unhappy into a story, you can overcome your depression more easily. Laughter is the best medicine.

Shortly after college I was feeling depressed about my

work. It seemed as if I would never be able to do everything I wanted to do. I went for a walk with a writer named Dan Jacobsen, who had been my creative writing teacher when I was a student at Syracuse University, and as we walked he told me a story.

BRING IN THE CHICKENS
Europe/Poland/Yiddish

Once, long ago in Poland, there was a man who felt depressed. He went to his rabbi to tell him his problems.

"Rabbi," the man said, "I am so unhappy."

"What is wrong?" said the rabbi.

"My house is so small. It only has one room. Not only do my wife and our five children live in it but also my mother-in-law. What can I do?"

"Bring the chickens into the house," said the rabbi.

The man went home and, because everyone knew the rabbi was a very wise man, he did as the rabbi said. A week later he came back to the rabbi.

"Rabbi," said the man, "it is worse with the chickens in the house. They squawk and flap around and dirty the floor. I am going to go crazy. What can I do?"

"Now," said the rabbi, "bring the pig into the house."

The man did as the rabbi said, but it was only four days later this time when he went back to the rabbi.

"Rabbi," he said, "I thought it was bad with the chickens, but now with the pig it is even worse. I am always tripping over it. And it tips over our table while we are eating. I cannot imagine that any man could have a life that is worse than mine. What can I do?"

"Hmm," said the rabbi. "Bring the cow into the house."

The man went home and did as the rabbi told him, but he was back the very next day.

"Rabbi," he said, "my house is like a barnyard. It is never quiet. There is no room to move now that the cow is in the house. I no longer worry about going crazy. I *am* crazy. Rabbi, I tell you, unless you can help me, I am going to go home now and drown myself in the well. What can I do?"

The rabbi smiled. "Ah," he said, "now take out the chickens."

That story Dan Jacobsen told me made me laugh. It also made me realize that as many troubles as I thought I had, things could always be worse. But if I just solved one of those problems, things would be better. To this day, whenever I feel overwhelmed, I only have to remember those words: "Now take out the chickens."

LESSON STORIES

Stories can help point the way out of our troubles. They can, in the very best way, teach lessons. By seeing how someone in a story overcomes his or her troubles, we can learn how to do the same.

Among Native American people, lesson stories are used as instruction and discipline in child rearing. When a child does something wrong, the child is told a lesson story by a parent or elder. The belief is that a story strengthens a child's mind and heart. Often, when a child misbehaves it is not because the child wishes to do wrong; it is because he or she is angry or confused. Telling a story with a very clear moral lesson is a way of healing confusion. If the child has been greedy or selfish, it may be a story about someone whose greedy, selfish behavior caused big trouble. A story that a child remembers will grow with that child throughout his or her life, even though the story may be as light as a feather's touch.

Lesson stories were not just told among Native Americans. They have been told all over the world to help not just children but all of us to learn the right ways to behave. The stories I tell throughout this book come from many different parts of the world and many different cultures. Look at any of the stories and see if you think they contain useful lessons. Do some of them contain more than one lesson? And how do those lessons work?

The stories of Yiyi the Spider are one example of lesson stories. Yiyi is both a spider and a person, the Ewe people say. He is much like Anansi the Spider, who is found in the stories of the Akan people of Nigeria. Many of those stories were brought by the Akan people to Jamaica, where the trickster is called Anancy. Stories of how Anancy sometimes tricks others and other times tricks himself are very popular in the West Indies.

In the United States many of the stories told by African Americans have their roots in the traditions of West Africa and the West Indies. In some places, Anancy stories became Aunt Nancy stories. In retelling the stories of Brer Rabbit, which are based on those remembered African folktales, the writer Joel Chandler Harris changed Aunt Nancy into the wise old slave Uncle Remus. The wisdom of those ancient stories made new in North America helped African Americans survive the time of slavery.

In many of the slave stories, characters who are physically weaker or in a position of relative powerlessness use their intelligence to overcome adversity. When Brer Rabbit outwits Brer Bear, who is big and strong but not very smart, it is like the slave outwitting his master. Virginia Hamilton's wonderful book *The People Could Fly* is a collection of such stories from the time of African American slavery. The title story tells of an old man who remembers how his people, back in Africa, could use their magical power to fly away from danger. The slaves on the plantation listen to his words, and as a result, they find their own wings and fly away from slavery. That story can be read as literal truth and also as a metaphor for the ability slaves had to use their wits and run away from slavery, taking the long road to freedom that led north to Canada, where slavery had been outlawed. As long as you remember that you were born to be free, the story tells us, you can never be kept as a slave.

However, you can also be a slave to your own faults. To African people one of the worst faults is greed. Here is one of the Yiyi the Spider stories that I learned while I was teaching in Ghana. It may sound familiar to you because one of the stories of Brer Rabbit has the same basic plot. It shows how a greedy person often causes his own downfall.

YIYI THE SPIDER AND THE STICK SAP MAN
Africa/Ghana/Ewe

Yiyi the Spider was a farmer. He had a big farm with all kinds of food growing on it. Yams, cassavas, breadfruit, peppers, tomatoes, orange trees, and pineapples all grew in his garden. He had a wife and many little children, but Yiyi was very greedy. He didn't want to share his garden with anyone. So, when night came, he sneaked out of the house and went to the garden and ate all the ripe fruit and vegetables.

The next day, when Yiyi and his wife and children went to the garden, they found that everything ripe was gone.

"Wo!" said Yiyi. "This is terrible. A thief has been in our garden. If I find who did this, I will beat him!"

Of course, Yiyi did not find the thief. And every night, he sneaked out to the garden and ate everything that was ripe.

Mrs. Spider was hungry and her many children were getting thin. So she went to her grandmother for help.

"A thief is stealing our food," said Mrs. Spider. "My poor husband, Yiyi, works so hard to feed us and then this happens. Yiyi has been trying to find the thief, but that thief is too tricky. What can we do?"

"Ey," said Mrs. Spider's grandmother. "The thief is tricky indeed. I am certain that Yiyi cannot catch this thief. I have a plan, though. But you must not tell your husband about it. This is a special plan for women only."

Mrs. Spider agreed. Then her grandmother told her what to do.

"Take these three sticks," she said. "Use them to gather three big balls of sticky sap from the trees," she said, "roll the sticks in the sap, and be careful not to touch it or you will get stuck."

Mrs. Spider did as her grandmother said. Then she and

her grandmother went to the garden in the evening after Yiyi had gone home. They stuck the three balls of sap together under a banana tree. They stuck two shiny stones in the ball on top, and those stones looked like eyes. They stuck a peanut in the middle, and it looked like a nose. They stuck a row of cowrie shells in, and they looked like teeth. They put one of Yiyi's old cloths around those balls of sticky sap, and now they looked like a real person.

"This will guard your farm," said Grandmother Spider.

That night, when everyone was sleeping, Yiyi slipped out of bed. He was hungry. He sneaked down to the garden, and he began to pick mangoes and papayas, coconuts and oranges, cassavas and yams, tomatoes and peppers. He made a great pile of those good things to eat.

"What have I forgotten to pick?" said Yiyi. "Ah, that is it. I need some bananas."

He went to the banana tree, but when he got there, he saw the stick sap man at the base of the tree. Yiyi jumped back, because he was startled.

"Who are you?" Yiyi said. But the stick sap man did not answer.

Now Yiyi became angry. "Why are you in my garden? Answer me."

But the stick sap man said nothing.

"If you do not answer me, I will punch you in the eye," said Yiyi.

Of course, the stick sap man said nothing. So Yiyi punched him in the eye. But Yiyi's hand stuck in that ball of sap.

"Let go of me," said Yiyi, "or I will punch you in the other eye."

Again, the stick sap man was silent, and Yiyi punched him in the other eye. Now both of Yiyi's hands were stuck.

"Stop grinning at me," said Yiyi, "or I will kick you."

But the cowrie-shell grin on the face of the stick sap man did not change, and when Yiyi kicked him, his foot became stuck, too.

"I will kick you again," said Yiyi. And he did so. Now both feet were stuck. All night Yiyi wrestled with the stick sap man, but he could not escape. When the next morning came, Yiyi's wife and their children and all the people in the village went to the farm. There they found Yiyi, caught by the stick sap man. A great pile of ripe fruit and vegetables was next to him.

"There is your thief," said Mrs. Spider's grandmother.

It took a long time to get Yiyi unstuck. Everyone was laughing and making fun of him. As soon as he was freed, Yiyi ran. He ran back home to his house. He was so ashamed when he got there that he jumped up into the highest, darkest corner of his house to hide. You will find Spider there to this day, hiding in the highest, darkest corners because of his shame.

TRANSFORMING ANGER, HEALING PAIN

I was taught by Native American elders that anger is really a twisting in the mind. When your mind is straight, you do not feel angry. Mental pain and deep sorrow can also be healed. If we look at the natural world, we will see that things are healthy when they are in balance. An elderly Iroquois friend of mine explained it in this way: "There is day and there is night," he said. There will always be darkness at the end of the day, but we don't need to be afraid of that darkness. It will always be followed by a new day's light. In the same way, there are days when the skies are clear and days when there is rain. With the right balance of light and darkness, of sun and rain, the plants will grow. If we maintain emotional balance, we will grow, too. There are always going to be things that make us angry or sad or confused. But knowing it is the way we are meant to be can help us try to find our way back to balance. Stories are like maps showing us the roads to follow in that healing journey.

I think one of the great problems we face in the world today is that we no longer understand how to transform our anger and heal our pain. Stories are one of the best ways to do both things—if they are the right stories. Stories can show us nonviolent ways to bring things back into balance. Through stories we may find that an enemy can become a friend. This story—which my friend Oren Lyons, a faith keeper of the Onondaga Nation of the Iroquois, told to me—is one such tale.

STRAIGHTENING THE MIND OF TADADAHO
North America/Northeast/Onondaga

Long ago there was a powerful chief of the Onondaga Nation. His name was Tadadaho. He would allow no man to stand against him, and everyone was afraid of him. His magic was so strong that he could make birds fall dead from the sky by speaking a single word. His love for power was so great it had twisted his body so that it had seven crooks in it. His thoughts were so twisted with anger that poisonous snakes grew from his hair.

In those days the five nations of the Iroquois were always at war with one another. Tadadaho was one of the greatest war leaders. Many died because of him. But there came a man called the Peacemaker. He said he was sent by the Creator to bring peace and happiness back to the people. His best friend was a man named Hiawatha, and the two of them went from one Iroquois nation to the next, speaking for peace. One by one the nations stopped fighting and embraced the idea of peace. The Seneca, the Cayuga, the Oneida, and the Mohawk people all listened to the Peacemaker and Hiawatha. They joined together in peace. Only the Onondaga, led by Tadadaho, still refused to accept peace.

The Peacemaker and Hiawatha tried to approach Tadadaho. He used his magic to escape them. Finally Hiawatha taught a song of peace to the people. Everyone sang that song. When Tadadaho heard the song of peace, it was so beautiful, he could only sit and listen. As he sat there, the Peacemaker and Hiawatha came up to him. They straightened his body. Then Hiawatha, whose name means "the comber," combed the snakes out of Tadadaho's hair.

Now that Tadadaho's mind was straight, he no longer felt anger and pain. He joined the league of peace. His great strength went into helping the cause. So Tadadaho, who had fought against peace, now became the leader of this new league of the five nations.

When we hear this story, it may remind us that those who seem to be capable of only doing bad may also be capable of doing good. It is also the kind of story to be told to someone who thinks that he or she is a terrible person. Sometimes, when we have done wrong, we can't see any way out of it. A story such as this one is very much like the New Testament stories in which men who were wrongdoers saw the light and changed their lives by following the teachings of Jesus. It can help people realize that they, too, can change their lives for the better.

Through our understanding, stories help us find ways to solve our problems. Often people turn to violence because they have never been shown a better way. For many years I have gone into prisons and youth detention centers to do storytelling workshops with the men and women who are locked behind bars because of their crimes. In youth facilities I find that many of the young people I work with come from broken families or have no family at all. They have joined gangs to find a kind of family they do not have at home.

Some of the people I work with are uncertain at first about hearing or telling stories. That changes quickly, though. Listening to stories gives them new ways to look at things. The truths in the stories I tell touch them. Telling their own stories helps them understand who they are and, also, who they might become.

I've been a student of the martial arts for a long time.

For six years I was an instructor of Pentjak-silat, the martial art of Indonesia. Studying the martial arts shouldn't make a person more violent but, instead, should help him or her discover the inner security and self-assurance to avoid violence. Because of that I find this next story, which I have often used working with people in prisons, especially moving.

A good friend of mine named John Stokes runs a program called the Tracking Project. It's designed to use the old skills of indigenous people, people who live close to the earth, to restore physical and mental balance. People are taught how to walk quietly in the woods, how to follow and understand the tracks they find there, how to build a fire with a bow drill, how to listen and understand the natural world around them and within them.

John studied for years in Australia with Aboriginal elders and has been working with native people in this country for two decades. John lives in New Mexico, and every year he does tracking workshops with young people in the various Indian pueblos around him. A few years ago, though, he went to a certain Native American high school and the principal told him that things at the school were not good.

"We have gangs here now," the principal said before they had an assembly to begin John's program at the school. "The kids are divided between Crips and Bloods. They've got guns. Yesterday we had our first gang shooting. I don't know if you're going to be able to do much with them."

"Well, let me try," John said.

That day, at the assembly, John saw that things had

changed at the school since he had been there last. The kids didn't look the way they had looked in past years. They wore sunglasses and bandannas with their gang colors on them. The kids in one gang sat on one side of the auditorium, and the kids in the other gang sat on the other side.

The principal opened the assembly. "I suppose you all heard that we had a shooting yesterday."

"That's right," one of the kids in the audience shouted back.

"It was because those guys flashed the bird. They were asking for it. They deserved to get shot," another kid yelled.

At this the principal began to cry. She turned and asked John to begin his program.

"You mean," John said to the kids, "they deserved to get shot because they made a rude gesture at someone."

"That's right," came back from the audience. More than one kid shouted that.

"You all agree?" John said.

"Yeah! Yeah!" Almost all the kids answered him.

"Then let me tell you a story," he said. Then John told this story, a story that both he and I had learned some years ago.

John told about a young American who spent many years studying the Japanese martial art of aikido. This young American became very skilled and was invited to study in Japan. He did well there, too. He thought he was becoming a Master.

One afternoon that young American got onto a train in the suburbs of Tokyo. He hadn't been on it long when a very big Japanese man got on. He started pushing and shoving other people on the bus. He cursed at them and threatened to hit them.

The young American smiled. He knew how to handle someone like that. The Japanese man was bigger than he was, but he would be able to take care of him in nothing flat. He reviewed in his mind the various things he would do when the man got to him. That man would learn what it was to tangle with a Master of the martial arts.

The big man continued down the aisle, cursing people, shoving them aside. It looked like he was going to start hurting people soon. The young American stood up. But before he could do anything, a very small elderly Japanese man called out in a friendly voice, "Hey! C'mere."

The big man went and stood in front of the old man.

The old man began to tell him a delightful story of being with his wife and watching the persimmon trees in their garden.

To the surprise of the young American, that big, rough man began to weep.

"I love persimmons, too . . . but my wife died," he sobbed. "I got no wife, no home, no job, no money. I'm so ashamed of myself."

The elderly man gently patted him on the shoulder. "It will be all right," said the old man. "It will be all right."

As the young American man sat back down, he realized how wrong he had been. He was not a Master. That old man was the Master.

———

When John Stokes finished his story, the whole auditorium was quiet. No one spoke. He looked out over the audience.

"Tomorrow," John said, "I'll be doing my workshops. But anyone who comes to them has to promise to do exactly what I tell them to do."

The next day, all of the kids who had been most involved in the gangs in that school were in John's workshops. They were there without their gang colors and without anger. And they opened their hearts and listened. They had understood the meaning of his story.

Catharsis is a word used by the ancient Greeks to describe the way people are affected after going to the theater and seeing a tragic story. By identifying with the people in the story, they experience those same deep emotions as the characters. Afterward that feeling of catharsis is a kind of emotional cleansing. You feel as if your troubles have been lightened, and you may see things more clearly than before. The story of these young people and John Stokes is an example of the cathartic power of story.

But Once a Year:
Stories about Celebration

Are there stories that you remember about a special time of year? A time when everyday things are put aside and something happens that can only happen then? Those times of celebration have their own kind of magic. There is a special kind of power in ritual. The act, for example, of bringing out a menorah and lighting the candles during Hanukkah has great meaning because it is done in the same way each year. Knowing that others have done this for thousands of years makes you feel part of that long history. Your life grows deeper and richer from being part of such traditions. These traditions always have stories connected to them, not only the old stories of how these yearly traditions came to be but also new stories that come from the experiences of each new generation.

Whether that special time is the coming of the Asian New Year or Kwanzaa or the Fourth of July or any of countless yearly celebrations, it will always have special memories connected to it. After all, those special times come but once a year. And what better way do we have than telling stories to hold on to and share those times? A story can look at an event from many different angles, let us hear many different voices.

Through stories your memories of those times of celebration can also be passed on to another generation. When I remember some of the stories that my grandmother told me about her own childhood, it seems as if I were there with her and her brothers. It seems as if, through her stories, her memories became my memories. Some of her favorite family stories were about times of celebration. Those stories were sometimes about the celebrations themselves. I remember her stories about Christmas. She told me about how they used to go out into the woods to cut their Christmas tree and how they made ornaments from popcorn and apples. She told me about the simple presents they got back then, sometimes things they themselves made for each other.

There are many different times of celebration. Some are very ancient, and many different people around the world share them. New Year's Eve, when most of the world welcomes the beginning of a new year, is one such celebration. Among Asians there is a special New Year that some people call Chinese New Year, although it is celebrated by more Asian peoples than just the Chinese.

Although these celebrations may have once been rooted in a particular religion, some of them are now only loosely connected to the original religious traditions from which they grew. The African diaspora—in which many different peoples of Africa were spread across the world during the time of slavery—has produced a number of celebrations that are international in tone. These yearly celebrations combine elements of African, European, and even Native American traditions. Mardi Gras in New Orleans and Carnival in the various West Indian islands and Brazil are celebrations that come out of this rich blending of cultures. In recent years a whole new celebration called Kwanzaa has been created for African Americans. Its purpose is to connect African Americans with African culture and to celebrate such things as pride, sharing, and community.

Some holidays or celebrations are only shared by everyone in the same country. For the United States, the Fourth of July is the most obvious example. Every country has its own special national holidays. Canada and the United States both celebrate Thanksgiving, but Canadian Thanksgiving is in October and the holiday is in November in the United States. Thanksgiving is a celebration that began in the

United States and brings together the traditions of two very different cultures. When the Pilgrims came to America, they were helped by the native people. The survival of the Plymouth colony depended on such Native Americans as Squanto, who spoke English and so could tell the newcomers what they needed to know about farming and gathering food in the new land. To celebrate their first successful harvest, the story goes, the Pilgrims gave a great feast and invited the Wampanoag Indians to join them. That is the tale of Thanksgiving time as told by the descendants of the Pilgrims and by most European Americans. Yet there is more than one way for this story to be told.

It can also be told from the point of view of Squanto. How was he able to speak English so well? It was because he had been captured and taken to England as a slave by Englishmen more than a decade before the coming of the *Mayflower*. He had managed to win his freedom and had come home all the way from England. But soon after his return, he was again taken captive and transported to Europe, where he was sold as a slave to a Spanish monk. Once again he spent years in captivity and then was able to return home. This time when he returned he found that his whole village was gone. Everyone had died from diseases brought by the English. The amazing thing, to me, about Squanto's story is that he still offered his help to the starving colonists after having been taken as a slave not once but twice. He helped them survive even though his own people had all died because of other English people.

Although European colonists first started celebrating

Thanksgiving in the early 1600s in what they renamed New England, they were doing something that had been done for a long time by the native people. Thanksgiving celebrations are very much a part of Native American life to this day. In fact, among the native people of the Northeast, there is more than one Thanksgiving.

The Iroquois people, for example, have more than a dozen celebrations of thankfulness. Each of these comes at a certain time of year and is marked by feasts and ceremonies. These thanksgiving celebrations include the Thanks to the Maple Festival, which comes in late winter when the maple trees are tapped for their sweet sap to make maple syrup; the Strawberry Thanksgiving in early summer, when that first red fruit is picked; and the Green Corn Festival in late summer, when the sweet corn is ready.

History, of course, is story. If it is well told, it comes alive for us and we feel as if we are there. But the way history is told depends upon who the storyteller is. Thanksgiving can mean something to Native Americans that it doesn't mean to most other Americans. I always enjoy hearing the same history told by different people. The more stories we know, the more we will know about the real facts of history.

Personal celebrations are special times unique to a particular person or family. Birthdays immediately come to mind, but there are other special times that individuals and families remember from year to year—such as anniversaries. These times almost always have stories connected to them.

You may have such stories or you might be able to make

up a story about one of those times of personal celebration. Try this. Tell a story about the best birthday you ever had. Think about all the things that made that time special. Then try doing the opposite. Tell a story about your worst birthday or the worst experience you've ever had connected to a birthday. Sometimes you may find that if the bad experience happened a long time ago, telling about it now will help you understand it. Painful memories may become less painful when you turn them into a story.

Remember your stories. They will help you remember who you are. They will help you see where you've been. They will help you find the way, wherever you are going.

ACTIVITIES

○ Smell different things—flowers, fruit, clothing, food—and see if they remind you of certain experiences.

○ Think of a time when you were very sad, frightened, or angry, and then remember what happened to make you feel happy.

○ Have a friend quickly tell you a story and see how much you can remember as you retell it. Be aware of the details you remember.

○ Have a parent or grandparent, an aunt or uncle tell you something about yourself when you were young, and try to remember that time and how you felt. Do you remember the situation the same or differently?

○ Read an article in the newspaper, or in a magazine, and see how much of the story you can remember in one sitting, then tell your recollection of the story to a friend.

○ Recall an event from the past—something funny, exciting, or scary—and discuss it with an old friend or relative who shared the experience. Consider how the two views differ.

○ Keep a journal or a diary of your dreams for a week, then find quiet time to think about them. Think about what the dreams tell you about yourself, your life, your feelings.

4

Imagine storytelling as a circle divided into four parts: The first part of that circle, where our storytelling journey began—*Listen.* When we listen, we hear stories being told all around us. The second part of that circle—*Observe.* With good observation, we can see many things that others do not see. A good storyteller has to be observant. The third part of the circle—*Remember.* Without memory, those things we've heard and seen will not remain with us. When we forget our stories, we may also forget who we are. All of this leads to the fourth part of the circle. *Share*—This is the part that brings it all together.

How do we share? Quite simply, we share by telling the stories we know to others. It has been said that elders—our grandparents, for example—are the ones whose primary job it is to share. In many parts of the world, very old people are regarded as treasures. Their knowledge of the past is useful in many ways. Have you ever noticed how your older relatives like to tell stories when there is a family gathering?

Sometimes those relatives, like my aunt Caroline, tell their stories again and again. You may even groan and say, "Oh no, here comes that same old story!" Remember, though, that those elderly relatives only tell the same stories again and again because those stories are important to them. There is some message in them that they want to share. They want to complete the circle.

Most people, not just young people but adults, also, seem to be too busy these days to listen to the stories elders want to share. One thing you can do, if you really want to be a storyteller, is to sit down and listen—really listen—to your older relatives who have stories to tell. You may be surprised at what they share with you.

And Now It's My Turn

Let's talk now about your own sharing. It's your turn to tell stories. How can you share the stories you've learned? Or perhaps we should ask first why you would want to share stories. To tell a story, you have to enjoy storytelling. Don't try to tell stories if doing so isn't fun for you. This isn't like a school assignment that you're required to complete. For me, storytelling is one of the best parts of my life. I get paid to do storytelling programs in schools and at festivals, but I could earn more money doing other things. I have a Ph.D. in literature and worked for many years as a college teacher and an administrator. I could have stayed in that profession. Instead, in 1981 I resigned my job. I chose to be a storyteller because it is what I love to do.

I love hearing new stories and old stories. People sometimes ask me who my favorite storyteller is. I always answer in the same way—I have too many favorite storytellers to be able to list them all. Every storyteller is different, and even the same story told by two different tellers doesn't sound the same. I love learning new stories to tell, and I love telling stories that I have known for many years. The sharing that is part of storytelling is one of the best parts of it all. To see people enjoying a story, living a story as I tell it, is one of the most exciting things in my life. So, if you don't like the idea of sharing stories, of telling them for others to hear, I advise you to find something else to do that brings joy into your life.

Everyone, at one time or another, is a storyteller. There are many occasions when we try to share things we've seen and heard with others by telling about those experiences. A good storyteller knows how to do this. Storytelling can be useful in many parts of your life. Very few people become professional storytellers, but almost everyone finds the communication skills of storytelling to be useful. Think of all the professions in which people use storytelling to do their job more effectively. When I think back on all the courses I took in grade school and high school and college, I realize many of the ones I loved the best were my favorites because the teacher knew how to tell stories.

When I was a college student at Cornell University, I led a busy life. I was a varsity heavyweight wrestler and also the editor of the school literary magazine. Sometimes I was too busy to go to every class. But one class that I never missed was comparative anatomy, taught by professor Perry

Gilbert. You never knew what story he was going to tell next in his class. It might be one of his famous stories about his adventures with sharks while he was skin-diving in the Caribbean; his story about the time a shark attacked him and grabbed his head in its jaws is a story I will *never* forget. Through stories, he made science come alive.

AROUND THE CAMPFIRE

If you still are not certain that storytelling is a part of your life, then let me remind you now of one more sort of story that I am certain you've heard or tried to tell—ghost stories! The Friday the 13th series of horror movies is based entirely on one popular scary story I first heard decades ago when I was at summer camp. That story told how campers were in danger of being murdered by the ghost of another camper who was accidentally killed at the same camp not long ago. I remember how nervously we all went back to our cabins after that campfire tale, even though we all kept saying things like "That wasn't true!" R. L. Stine's *Goosebumps* books also draw on that old tradition of telling scary tales.

I often travel to schools and do workshops in storytelling. One of the favorite parts of those workshops for many of the kids is when we come to ghost stories. I tell them one or two ghost stories I've learned over the years. Then I ask them if there are any ghost stories about their town or neighborhood. I send them home to ask around, and when we next meet I always hear some of the same stories that are told everywhere—like the tale of the hook found hanging on the door of a car by two kids who were parking late at night on a deserted back road but then sped off when they heard on the radio that a one-armed murderer with a hook for a hand had been seen near the place where they were parked. That story even turned up being told by Bill Murray in the movie *Meatballs*. But I also hear new stories, ones I've never heard before. Here's one of those stories.

THE SEVENTH BOY
North America/Northeast/Mohawk

There is a mausoleum that sits next to a small lake behind the old deserted castle called Beardsley Manor in Little Falls, New York. In the early 1900s the Beardsley family had been very wealthy. The Beardsleys were so wealthy that they had bought that castle in Ireland, had taken it apart, and had it shipped to America, where it was put back together stone by stone.

But all of the members of the Beardsley family passed away. It was said that their castle had been rebuilt on an unlucky spot. (There had been an Iroquois graveyard there long ago. Then a colonial fort was built there, though the fort was destroyed during a battle when a flaming arrow landed in the powder house and blew the whole thing sky-high.) All that was left was their deserted castle, the small, dark lake, and their stone mausoleum, in which the bones of the Beardsleys had been placed.

Strange things happened in Beardsley Manor and around the lake. This is the story of the mausoleum.

One night a group of seven high school boys got together. They wanted to find a deserted place for a party.

"Let's go to the old mausoleum," one of them said.

Some of the boys didn't like the idea, but the other boys dared them.

"Are you chicken?" they taunted.

When they got to the mausoleum, they saw that the door to it was locked. But one of the boys found an iron bar and used it to break the lock. They opened the big, creaking door and went in . . . all but one boy, who refused.

"It's not right to disturb the dead," he said. And he turned around and walked home.

The other six boys didn't mind. "We're not chicken," they said. Then they decided to see if anything was in the caskets they found in the corner of one room. They opened them up, every one of them. And they found bones. The bones of the Beardsleys.

They kept daring each other to do things.

"Dare you to open that casket."

"Dare you to pick up that skull."

"Dare you to throw those bones in the lake."

Finally it was very late. They headed for home. One boy took a skull as a souvenir. Another one took a foot bone. Another one took an arm bone. Another took a leg bone. Nothing happened to any of them that night.

But the next week the boy who had taken the skull had an accident. He fell off his bike and died of a fractured skull. A week after that the boy who had taken the foot bone stepped on a rusty nail, got tetanus, and died. One after another, every single one of those six boys died. None of them escaped the Beardsley Curse. The only one to survive was the seventh boy, who had said it was wrong to disturb the dead and then had gone home.

This story was told to me by a fourth-grade girl in Little Falls Elementary School in New York. She said she'd heard the story from her dad. She told the story so well that we decided to have her tell it again in the final program at the end of the week. Lots of parents came to that assembly, and everyone agreed that her story was the best. After the assembly she introduced me to her parents.

"That was some story," I said to her father as I shook his hand. "Your daughter says you were the one who taught it to her."

"That's right," he said. He was a tall, quiet-looking man, and something about the way he said that made me ask a further question.

"Where'd you learn that story?" I said. "I'd like to tell it to people, too, but I'd like to know its source."

He paused for a moment and then he answered me. "I was the seventh boy," he said. "You can tell it all you like. Just don't mention our names."

Imagine yourself sitting around a campfire. Your camp counselor has just finished telling a ghost story. Think of how the unexpected and the expected blend together to make a ghost story effective. Think of how almost every ghost story revolves around someone doing something they shouldn't have done. Now can you share a scary story of your own with everyone?

The Act of Storytelling

What are the stories you can tell? Your own stories are a good place to start. I've spoken in the earlier chapters about how to find your own stories. I always suggest to people who are starting out as storytellers that they should find their own stories, stories that come from their storytelling roots. Often those stories are just as interesting for others to hear as stories you take from a book or hear from another storyteller. Also, your own stories may be unique. Because they are your stories, you can tell them in a way no one else can. Because they are yours, you will probably be more comfortable telling them.

However, it is also true that stories are meant to be shared. Storytellers are always trading stories with one another. Many of the stories I tell were told to me by someone else. I have also read many collections of stories and sometimes adapt those written stories to oral telling. But who owns those stories? If those stories belong to someone else, if they are in a book that is copyrighted or are being told by a professional storyteller, can you tell them? What are the rules?

Because storytelling has become so popular so quickly, many people are still uncertain about this. There is an unwritten agreement among storytellers that they will not "steal" stories from one another. Whenever they hear another storyteller tell a story that they want to tell themselves, they ask that storyteller for his or her permission to tell the story. I have done this on a number of occasions. I often get visits or phone calls from other storytellers who have heard me tell a certain story or read a version of it published in one of my books.

Asking permission is a good thing to do. Not only is it right to get someone's permission before using his or her story, there may be things about that story you need to know. A story can be like an iceberg—only part of it is visible when it is told. When I tell stories about the Abenaki hero named Gluskabe, I don't tell everything about him or everything about Abenaki culture in each story. But there are things that I know, things that I think any storyteller should know to tell a Gluskabe story. In one story Gluskabe travels with his two dogs. One of them is white and one is black. If the story was told by someone else and the storyteller decided to change the color of the dogs, he or she would be making a big mistake. It is understood in Abenaki culture (though it isn't explained in that particular story) that those two dogs are wolves. The black wolf stands for the night while the white wolf stands for the day.

Whenever I give anyone permission to tell Gluskabe stories, I always give background information like that. I also tell how to pronounce the Abenaki words in the stories and explain the meaning of those words. *Gluskabe*, for example, is pronounced Gloos-kah-bey. It can be translated as "the talking person" or "the storyteller." I was taught this by Stephen Laurent, an Abenaki elder.

If you learn a story from someone else, whether it is a written version or an oral telling, you should always give credit. When you tell the story, say who the story comes from. Mention his or her name or the name of the book. You may have noticed how I have done that throughout this book.

David Holt and Bill Mooney recently published a

wonderful book called *Ready-to-Tell Tales,* stories told by some of America's favorite storytellers with tips about how to tell each story. Those stories are all offered to anyone who wishes to learn them and tell them. At the start of their book, David Holt and Bill Mooney point out that when you tell one of the tales from their book, you should tell a little about the teller you got it from because "in this way we lift each other up, one story at a time."

HOW TO TELL

Knowing a story is only half of what makes someone a storyteller. Telling the story, being able to effectively share it, is the other half. No storyteller knows everything about storytelling. Every good storyteller will tell you that he or she is still learning things, even after many years of storytelling. However, here are some things that can be useful to you— a few tips on how to tell a story.

When you choose a story to tell, make sure that story is right for you. Ask yourself a few simple questions: Why do I want to tell this story? What do I like about it? If someone asked me what the story is about, could I explain it? Can I really see this story when I tell it? If you can answer those questions, that story may be right for you.

You can also ask yourself about the right time to tell the story. A good storyteller knows more than one story and will choose a story that is right for the moment. That moment might be a public performance or a time when you need to communicate something to someone else. Your audience might be a hundred people or one person. Again, ask yourself some questions: Is this a story my audience will understand? Is this the right story to tell now? Why is it the right story to tell? How do I hope my audience will respond to this story? Think, for example, of the story John Stokes chose to tell to the students in that high school assembly. Wasn't that the right story to tell at that time? Think of other stories that would not have worked in that setting.

A story is like a walk on a familiar path. You know all the landmarks. You know where it begins, and you know where to turn at the right times. But you don't remember every single step you take. People sometimes make the mistake of thinking they have to memorize every word to tell a story. Memorizing a story word-for-word is not the way that professional storytellers do it. Instead, they know the heart of the story and then tell it in their own words. Try to see your story as you tell it.

Martha Hamilton and Mitch Weiss are two storytellers who call themselves Beauty and the Beast. (They refuse to say which of them is Beauty and which is the Beast, though!) They have helped kids tell stories for so many years that they finally put together a book called *Children Tell Stories*. It is intended as a guide for teachers, but it's a book useful for any storyteller, young or old. They offer great tips on learning stories. They suggest making up a pictorial outline in which you draw each of the important scenes in the story. The pictures don't have to be great ones. It's just a way to help you visualize—really *see*—your story. Once you've done that, the scenes of the story are firmer in your memory.

One of the most common mistakes a beginning storyteller can make is hurrying. Beginners think they have to tell a story as fast as they can before they forget it. They get so nervous that their words explode out of them. Remember, *there is no hurry in storytelling.* A story is not a hundred-yard dash. Take a deep breath before you start, and then breathe normally as you tell the story.

Don't tell a story as if it is one long, long sentence. Stop now and then. Pause appropriately. When you have said something that makes people laugh, wait until the laughter stops before you continue. If you are coming to a scary moment, it sometimes helps to pause for a few seconds before going on. This builds suspense. If you want to be sure you are pausing, try this: When you want to have a pause, stop talking and then count silently, "One and one thousand, two and one thousand, three and one thousand." That will be a three-second pause. Don't be afraid of silence in a story. It is important to give the listener time to absorb the story. Silence can help.

You don't have to go slow all the time, of course. The pace of your story can speed up at times when quickness is right—perhaps one of the characters in your story is running away from something. Varying the pace can make a story much more interesting to hear.

Another common mistake made by beginning storytellers is to tell the story in a voice that no one can understand. They mumble their words or speak so softly that no one can hear them. Speak clearly. Some storytellers do vocal exercises to warm up before they tell. They find a place where they can be alone and then they do the scales: do, re, mi, fa, so, la, ti, do. Or they do other vocal exercises of the sort that singers do. I never do this myself, but many people find it useful. Find out what works for you.

When you speak, speak from the diaphragm. The diaphragm is located in the center of your body, just below your ribs. Put your hand there and feel how your diaphragm pushes your stomach out as you breathe in. If you speak from your throat only, your voice is weak. If you think of speaking from your diaphragm, your voice grows stronger and can be heard farther away. This is called projecting. Remember, when you tell a story, you want everyone in the room to hear—especially those people far in the back.

Don't think you have to sound like anyone else when you tell a story. You can always learn from listening to other storytellers. However, imitating someone else is difficult. Use your own voice when you tell a story. There are storytellers with southern accents, with New York City accents, with accents from Britain, the Caribbean, and India. All of those storytellers speak English, and their stories can be understood by anyone who speaks English. Yet they all tell in their own voices, with their own accents.

You can also decide whether you want to change the sound of your voice—tone, pitch, volume. Can you make your voice sound sad? Can you make it sound happy or frightened? Choosing the right time to change your voice in those ways is important in storytelling. Do you want to make your voice different for each character in your story? If you do, make sure that you choose the right sound. A mouse usually doesn't sound like a moose. An old man usually doesn't sound like a little girl. And don't make the mistake of using the wrong voice for the wrong character. Red Riding Hood should not sound like the Big Bad Wolf! It might be best when you start telling stories to just let the story itself tell about those various characters rather than trying to change your voice to fit each different character. Again, as always, find out what works for you.

I've already mentioned such things as the tone of your voice, its loudness or softness. But there are other things you can use as a storyteller. One example is facial expressions. We say a lot to each other without words.

Try this exercise, which requires at least three people. Make up a list of words for moods: happy, sad, angry, confused, frightened, disgusted, shy, self-confident. Write each of these words on a card.

Person #1 faces person #2.

Person #3, with the cards, stands behind person #2.

Person #3 holds up a card so that only person #1 can see it.

Then, using *only facial expressions,* person #1 tries to look as if he or she is in the mood noted on the card.

Person #2, who can't see the card, has to guess what that mood is.

Gesture and body movement are also part of the unspoken language we use every day. If someone holds up a hand, palm facing you as you are approaching, you stop. That gesture is as easily understood as the opposite gesture, in which a person moves one hand toward himself or herself with the palm facing his or her own chest. That means "Come here."

A few well-chosen gestures can be very useful in a story. Do not overdo it, however. If you swing your arms so much that you look like a windmill, you may distract your audience from the story you are telling. I often use American Indian sign language in my storytelling. I began to learn it many years ago from a Pueblo/Apache storyteller named Swift Eagle. Swifty, as his friends called him, used sign language all the time. As he spoke, his hands would make the signs for his words. If you are going to use hand gestures or sign language of any kind, it helps to practice in front of a mirror; then you can get an idea of what your audience will see. (Remember, though, you never see yourself in a mirror exactly as others see you.)

Storytelling is an art that you cannot really learn from books. Books tell you about it. They can offer suggestions on how to do it. But storytelling is something you can only learn by doing. The real learning comes when you start telling stories. You may have to tell a story a dozen times before you finally tell it right. Some storytellers practice a story for many months before they ever tell it in public. Don't worry and don't hurry. Just do it because you enjoy doing it. Do it and then do it again.

Writing Stories

A written story and a told story are similar, but they are not the same. They can work together, though. One can tell you about the other. For many years I have been writing down the stories I tell. In addition to writing down traditional stories you have heard from others, you can also do creative writing. You can write down your own stories. You can also write stories that come completely from your imagination, stories that have never been told before. The more stories you know, the easier it will be to imagine new stories.

When you are writing a story, it helps to read aloud what you have written. Read it aloud to yourself or to a friend. Listen and see if it sounds stiff or if it sounds like a living voice. Even more importantly, does it sound like *your* voice? A good writer always has a distinctive voice, something that makes you want to read or listen to that writer.

You may find, however, that the words you write on the page do not work the same in the story when it is told. The written versions of my stories do not contain everything I share with my audiences when I am telling. Many of the things I just spoke about—tone, pitch, gesture, body language—can only be found in the performance of a story.

Even an audiotape or a videotape does not capture everything in a live performance. The presence of the actual living storyteller is important; the direct contact between a storyteller and an audience is lost in a recording. I always point out that when we are all in a room together, we are sharing our breath. The air we breathe out is the air that the others in the room breathe in. Stories are carried by our breath, and so we are breathing in those stories when we hear a live storytelling performance.

Things to Help Remembering

Storytellers the world over have long used physical objects to help them remember stories. Those objects are called mnemonic devices. Not only do they help you, they are interesting for the audience to see. Pictures, photographs, knotted ropes, carved sticks, quilts with designs on them—there are all kinds of mnemonic devices. For instance, Native American people in the Northeast had two mnemonic devices that I use. Those devices are wampum and a storytelling bag.

Wampum: The word *wampum* comes from the Narragansett word *wampum-peag,* meaning "white strings." Wampum was originally made of small white shells that were strung together to form patterns. Those patterns symbolized important events or agreements. When someone who knew the history of those agreements or events looked at the wampum, that person could then "read" the story. In a way, a wampum belt was the same as a treaty or a legal document. It also recorded important stories.

When the Europeans came, they learned how important wampum was. They began to sell white and purple beads to the native people, and those beads were strung together to make even more intricate wampum belts. In some cases, European nations made wampum belts and gave them to native nations to symbolize and ratify agreements between them. Later on, wampum was sometimes used like money between those early European settlers and native people. But using wampum to barter was a secondary use.

I carry a wampum belt with me called the Gluskabe Belt. Here is a picture of it.

There are many stories held in this belt. Whenever I use this belt to tell one of the stories that it contains, I hold it up and point to each of the designs on the belt in turn. At the appropriate times in telling the story, I also point to the four directions, move my hand across in a wavery fashion to stand for the winds, and point to my ears, eyes, nose, and mouth.

THE CREATION OF GLUSKABE
North America/Northeast/Abenaki

This is the story of how Gluskabe, the first storyteller, was created. The white cross in the center of my wampum belt stands for the four directions. It also stands for the way Gluskabe was created. He was shaped out of the earth. His head was toward the Dawn, his feet toward the Sunset. His right arm was toward the Winter Land. His left arm was toward the Summer Land.

The four crosses around him, each with a hole in the center, stand for the four winds that were sent then by Ktsi Nwaskw, the Great Mystery. Those winds blew and gave the breath of life to Gluskabe. But although Gluskabe had a head, he did not yet have any holes in it. So the Great Mystery made the lightning strike seven times. The seven slanted lines to the side of my wampum belt stand for those lightning strokes. Two lightning strikes made Gluskabe's two ears. Now he could listen to both sides. Two more lightning strikes made Gluskabe's two eyes. Now he could see the things close to him and the things far away. Two more made his nostrils. Now he could smell things that smelled good and things that smelled bad. Then one last lightning strike made his mouth. Although Gluskabe was given two ears, two eyes, and two nostrils, only one mouth was needed. It reminded him that he needed to listen and observe and smell the world around him twice as much as he talked about it. It is a lesson that all storytellers everywhere need to remember.

The Storytelling Bag: The storytelling bag was a leather bag with a drawstring top. It was usually deep enough to let you put your whole hand into it and feel around for the objects inside. Iroquois and Abenaki storytellers often carried those bags. When they had gathered the people around them, they might open their bag and hold it out to the audience.

"Reach in and pull out a story," they would say.

Then someone would reach deep into the bag and pull something out. It might be a crow feather. If so, then the storyteller would tell one of the stories about Crow—perhaps the story of how his feathers were turned black. It might be a small stone hatchet. If so, then the storyteller might tell the story of how the hero Skunny-Wundy used his tiny hatchet to defeat the great stone giant. Each of the many things in that bag symbolized a story.

You can make your own storytelling bag. Each time you learn a story, make some small object—that will not break easily—and place it in your storytelling bag. Part of the fun of this is not knowing what story you will tell until you pull an object from the bag.

I have seen some of the mnemonic devices used by story-tellers in other parts of the world. In Australia, storytellers sometimes make marks in the sand as they tell their stories. Cat's cradles of string or yarn are used in many places to tell stories, including throughout Europe and the British Isles, in Papua New Guinea, and among the Inuit people of the Far North. The Hmong people of Southeast Asia make tap-estries with the pictures and words of stories embroidered onto them in brightly colored thread. In Africa, among the Sambul people of Angola, storytellers use a storytelling vine. The storyteller ties small things to a vine that grows near his or her house. Each object stands for a story. This is not just done in Angola but also in Zaire, in Congo Kinshasa, and in many other parts of western, southern, and central Africa. I have seen African storytelling vines with tiny brooms, tin cans, pieces of clothing, wooden dolls, fishhooks, animal bones, and all sorts of things attached to them.

Here, too, each object stands for a different story. In this case, those who wanted to hear a story had to point to a particular object on the vine for that story to be told. It was also customary to give the storyteller a gift for each story that was shared.

You may want to try making your own memory devices for storytelling. You can use a piece of string or a grapevine to make a storytelling vine. Because the objects on a story-telling vine don't rattle around together in the bottom of a pouch, you can put things that are more fragile and delicate on your storytelling vine. A cloth or leather bag can be used as a storytelling bag. And to make your own story tapestry, you can either sew different patches of cloth together and embroider on them or draw pictures on them with different colored markers. All of these things, whether you use them or not in telling your stories, can help you to see your stories more clearly and to plant those stories more deeply in your memory.

Telling It to the Trees: It also helps to hear things more than once—and when you have heard a story that you would like to tell, to write it down for yourself. To memorize a story, don't try to remember it word-for-word. Remember the main points in the story. Then tell the story aloud to yourself. Do it more than once.

A storyteller friend of mine named Jeanine Laverty sometimes helps others learn to be storytellers. She knows that when you first begin telling stories, you are sometimes self-conscious about telling them out loud to other people. One of the things she suggests you can do to learn how to remember and tell stories is to go out into the woods and find a friendly-looking tree. Then tell your story aloud to that tree! The great thing about tree-telling is that trees never get bored and walk away. And no tree has ever corrected anyone who has made a mistake. Trees are very forgiving. Try it—you will soon see.

Involving Your Audience

It is important to make storytelling a shared experience. Your audience needs to feel it is part of the circle your story has shaped. Good telling will do that.

Eye Contact: Keeping eye contact is another way. Pick out several friendly-looking people in different parts of your audience. As you tell your story, look at one of those people as you talk. Tell the story to that person. When you have told a good part of your story, perhaps a quarter of the tale, switch your eye contact to another person on the other side of the room. It's good to find people who are really responsive to your story, people who seem to be listening intently. If you continue doing this, everyone in your audience will feel that you are looking at and care about him or her.

Ho? Hey! You also need to make sure your audience is awake and listening. Sometimes when I do programs in schools, it takes a while for the energy in the room to settle down. You probably know how it is in a school assembly. Kids have things on their minds other than the speaker. They're talking to friends, noticing who is sitting where, thinking about things they have to do that day. Maybe they're worried about a test they forgot to study for or thinking that they wore the wrong clothes.

I have one traditional way of drawing the focus of a room to the story. It's a device used by Native American storytellers here in the Northeast, especially the Abenaki and Iroquois people. I introduce it like this:

Long ago, these stories were told in wigwams and longhouses in the wintertime, late at night around a fire. You know how easy it is to go to sleep at night when you are sitting around a fire, don't you? But when a story is told, people have to be awake and listening. They have to have their eyes and ears open. So this is what we used to do to make sure everyone was awake. Every now and then, the storyteller would say, Ho? *Then, everyone who was awake and listening would say back,* Hey! *And that is what I am going to do.*

Ho?

That first *Ho?* is always answered at least a few times by *Hey!* But I do it again until everyone in the room is answering. Every now and then I call out "Ho?" as I tell my story. Because people know it is coming but they don't know when, they are alert and waiting for it. Saying it also sometimes wakes up people in the audience who have fallen asleep, or brings back the attention of those whose minds are wandering.

Devices like *Ho?* and *Hey!* call-and-response words are used in many different cultures. In Haiti the words used are *Krik?* and *Krak!* You may want to use *Ho?* and *Hey!* or you may want to find other words that are used in your own tradition. You may even want to make up words of your own to use this way.

Songs in Stories and Stories in Song: Another very effective way to involve your audience is through singing. There are many songs that are actually stories. Those songs have a chorus, which everyone sings together. Or they may simply repeat the last line of each stanza, with the storyteller singing it the first time and everyone singing along the second time.

There are also stories that have songs within them. Bessie Jones, an African American storyteller from the Georgia Sea Islands, tells many such stories. I remember one story in which children call their dogs to help them when they are in trouble. The chorus, which everybody sings together, goes like this:

> *Sue Boy and Doodley Doo,*
> *Your master is calling you . . .*

Here is a storytelling song that is based on tall tales. It's called "The Ballad of the Frozen Logger." In each stanza the last line is a sing-along. I learned it first from Lawrence Older, an Adirondack musician and storyteller who lived only four miles from the little general store my grandparents ran. When I was a small child, people like Lawrence Older used to come to the store, sit around the stove, and tell stories and sing songs such as this one. One word may need to be explained. A *mackinaw* is a woolen coat worn in very cold weather.

THE BALLAD OF THE FROZEN LOGGER

North America/Northeast/Adirondack

While I was in a truck stop, 'twas on a Saturday,
A thirty-year-old waitress to me these words did say:
"I see you are a logger and not just a common bum,
For nobody but a logger stirs his coffee with his thumb.

"My lover was a logger and a good one they say.
If you poured gravy on it, he'd eat a bale of hay.
The whiskers were so stubborn upon his leathery hide,
He would drive them in with a hammer and bite them off
  inside.

"My lover came to see me upon a wintry day.
He held me in his fond embrace and broke three vertebrae.
He kissed me as he was leaving, so hard he broke my jaw,
And I could not speak to warn him, he forgot his
  mackinaw.

"I watched him as he was leaving, he whistled as he did
  go,
Just striding through the snowdrifts at forty-eight below.
The weather tried to freeze him, it tried its level best.
At a hundred degrees below zero, he buttoned up his vest.

"But it froze clear down to China, it froze to the stars
  above.
At a thousand degrees below zero, it froze my logger love.
They tried their best to save him, if you believe me, sir.
They made him into ax blades to cut the mighty fir.

"And so I lost my lover and to this café I come,
And here I wait till someone stirs his coffee with his
thumb."

Whether you sing your stories or tell them, you'll find that sharing a story will make the story even more fun for you. The best part of it all is that when you complete the circle by sharing a story, others will usually share their stories with you. Then the circle starts all over again.

Activities

O   Sit with a friend or relative and talk about your day.

O   Sit with a friend or relative and share what you have read or seen that day.

O   Sit in a room at your home with friends and/or relatives and have them ask you what different things in the room mean to you. Then visit your friends and/or relatives at their homes and ask them the same question.

O   Recall an event from the past—something funny, exciting, or scary—and discuss it with an old friend or relative who shared the experience. Consider how the two views differ.

O   Call up a friend or relative you have not spoken with for a while and share your feelings about recent events.

O   Sit with friends and/or relatives and tell one of your favorite stories.

5

THE CIRCLE CONTINUES

The circle, of course, does not end. When you have gone all the way around it, you just begin again. That is the way with stories. They are always going around. There are always new stories being told and old stories being told anew.

Sometimes the same story is told in many places or in many ways. As you learn more about storytelling, you'll find there are motifs that are repeated again and again in stories. The fool who is smarter than the so-called wise person, the boy or girl who goes out to seek his or her fortune, the magical flight, the animal that helps a person in distress— these are only a few of hundreds of motifs found in stories. But it is not the motif that makes a story work. It is how and when the story is told that is more important.

It is also true that as we start around the circle again, we discover that young people often have as much to teach as their elders do. We can learn from the young as well as the old.

Handsome Lake, an Iroquois prophet of the early 1800s,

said that parents should always listen to the words of their children. The part of the circle where things begin again is a very strong place.

Here are two stories about the wisdom of youth to complete this book and start the circle over again.

The first story is one that seems to be popular all over the world. I have heard it told in many places. I've heard versions of it told in central Europe, in Africa and Asia, and among Native American people. Maggie Pierce of Northern Ireland tells this story in *Ready-to-Tell Tales* as "The Story of the Half Blanket." I first learned it from a telling by Carolee Jacobs, a Mohawk storyteller (who learned it from her mother), as "Sha-Tewahsiri:Hen," which means "Half a Blanket." Here is my version of the story.

THE OTHER HALF OF THE BLANKET
North America/Northeastern Canada/Mohawk

Onen. Now, here is my story. Long ago there was a man whose father had grown very old. This man lived with his wife and his son in a small lodge, and he grew tired of having to take care of the old man. The old man was too old and weak to work. What use was it to have him around? So, one day, he decided it was time for the old man to go. He called his son, who was only eight winters old, to him.

"It is time to take your grandfather into the forest and leave him there," the man said. He picked up a blanket and handed it to the boy. "Wrap this around your grandfather's shoulders when you leave him in the forest."

The boy did not say a word. He took the blanket and then led his grandfather out into the forest. Then he tore the blanket in half. He wrapped half of it around his grandfather's thin shoulders and brought the other half of the blanket back with him.

When he walked into the lodge, the man saw what his son was carrying.

"Why did you bring back half of the blanket?" he said.

"When you get old," the boy said, "I'll wrap this half of the blanket around your shoulders when I leave you in the forest."

For a moment the man did not know what to say. Then he nodded.

"Ah," said the man. "I understand. Son, I am sorry. I was wrong. Go into the forest and bring your grandfather back home."

Until the early part of this century, there was a tradition in Japan of public storytellers. These men, called *kataribe* in Japanese, traveled around the countryside telling their tales, most of which come from the Tokugawa period of Japanese history (1603–1867). Most of these stories have never been translated into English. The following story, about the three young crows and the archer, is my own telling of one of those tales, adapted from a version published thirty years ago in a book called *Tales from the Japanese Storytellers*, edited by Harold Henderson.

THE THREE YOUNG CROWS
Asia/Japan/Japanese

One day a flock of crows gathered in the forest. The life of a crow is not easy. To survive requires wisdom. So, Old Crow, who was leader of the flock, decided to test three fledglings to see if they were wise enough to become part of the flock.

"Tell me," said Old Crow to the first young one, "of all things in the world below us, what is the most dangerous?"

"An arrow," said the first young crow.

All of the crows in the flock flapped their wings in approval. *Hata-taki, hata-taki.*

"That is wise," said Old Crow. "You may join the flock."

Then he turned to the second young one. "What is your answer?" he asked.

"A skillful archer is the most dangerous thing. Without a skillful archer to shoot it, an arrow is no more dangerous than this branch on which I am sitting."

All of the crows in the flock cawed their approval. *Ka-a-ka-a, ka-a-ka-a.*

"That is even wiser," said Old Crow. "You, too, may join the flock."

Then he turned to the last one, who had sat silently while the others spoke.

"What do you say?" said Old Crow to the third young crow.

"I say that the most dangerous thing in the world below is an archer who is not skillful," said the little crow.

All of the other crows were shocked. They did not caw or flap their wings because they could not understand this answer.

"What do you mean by that?" said Old Crow, scratching his head in confusion.

"The answer is easy," said the third young crow. "When a skillful archer shoots at you, you only have to listen for the twang of the bowstring. Then, if you flit to one side or another, the arrow will miss you. But when you hear the twang of the bowstring of an unskillful archer, you do not know whether it is safer to sit still or to fly."

At that, all of the crows in the flock bowed their heads to this young one who knew so much.

Old Crow bowed his head, too. "Your answer is the wisest of them all," he said. "You will not just join our flock. You will be our leader."

And so it was.

There are many ways to end a story. One of the most familiar endings is "...and they all lived happily after." However, even though one story may end, there will always be another story to hear or another tale to tell. Wherever you go, stories will be there to meet you. May your journey be a long and happy one. As we say in Abenaki—*Wlipamkaani, nidoba.* Travel well, my friend.

Additional Resources

Brody, Ed, Jay Goldspinner, Katie Green, Rona Leventhal, and John Porcino, eds. *Spinning Tales, Weaving Hope: Stories, Storytelling and Activities for Peace, Justice and the Environment.* Philadelphia: New Society Publishers, 1992.

Hamilton, Martha, and Mitch Weiss. *Children Tell Stories: A Teaching Guide.* Katonah, New York: Richard C. Owen Publishers, 1990.

Harrison, Annette. *Easy-to-Tell Stories for Young Children.* Jonesborough, Tennessee: National Association for the Preservation and Perpetuation of Storytelling, 1992.

Holt, David, and Bill Mooney, eds. *Ready-to-Tell Tales: Surefire Stories from America's Favorite Storytellers.* Little Rock, Arkansas: August House Publishers, Inc., 1994.

Justice, Jennifer, ed. *The Ghost and I: Scary Stories for Participatory Telling.* Cambridge, Massachusetts: Yellow Moon Press, 1992.

Livo, Norma J., and Sandra A. Rietz. *Storytelling Activities.* Englewood, Colorado: Libraries Unlimited, Inc., 1987.

Pellowski, Anne. *The Story Vine: A Source Book of Unusual and Easy-to-Tell Stories from around the World.* New York: Simon & Schuster, Inc., 1984.

Storytelling Magazine is another great resource. The quarterly magazine is published by the National Storytelling Association, P.O. Box 309, Jonesborough, Tennessee 37659. The National Storytelling Association has a mail-order catalog, publishes many storytelling books, and sponsors a storytelling festival in Jonesborough every October.